SEDUCTION OF THE INNOCENT

Brother Francis had come from his holy quarters in Italy to give warning of the devil in human form who called himself Damien Thorn II.

He tried to tell the beautiful woman journalist, Anna Brompton. But she mocked his warnings, while Francis rejected the wave of lust that had unaccountably swept over him.

Only when he reached his room did he begin to feel safe from those strange and terrible stirrings. Then he sensed he was not alone. Muttering a prayer, he reached for his crucifix. But when he touched it, he felt the texture of skin.

Then he saw them. Anna lay on his bed, a young man on top of her. Both were naked, the young man thrusting at her furiously. When they saw him, they did not stop. Instead Anna smiled at Francis, and urged him to join them. . . .

THE ABOMINATION
Never underestimate the power of evil!

Great Horror Fiction from SIGNET

*Prices slightly higher in Canada
†Not available in Canada

OMEN V

THE ABOMINATION

GORDON McGILL

A SIGNET BOOK

NEW AMERICAN LIBRARY

PUBLISHER'S NOTE

This novel is a work of fiction. Names, characters, places, and incidents either are the product of the author's imagination or are used fictitiously, and any resemblance to actual persons, living or dead, events, or locales is entirely coincidental.

Copyright © 1985 by Twentieth Century-Fox Film Corporation

SIGNET TRADEMARK REG. U.S. PAT. OFF. AND FOREIGN COUNTRIES
REGISTERED TRADEMARK—MARCA REGISTRADA
HECHO EN CHICAGO, U.S.A.

SIGNET, SIGNET CLASSIC, MENTOR, PLUME, MERIDIAN and NAL BOOKS
are published by New American Library,
1633 Broadway, New York, New York 10019

First Printing, July, 1985

1 2 3 4 5 6 7 8 9

PRINTED IN THE UNITED STATES OF AMERICA

And . . . Satan shall be loosed out of his prison and shall go out to deceive the nations which are in the four corners of the earth, Gog and Magog, to gather them together to battle: the number of whom is as the sand of the sea.

REVELATION 20: 7-8

IN MEMORIAM:

Chessa Whyte
Father Edgardo Emilio Tassone
Kathy Thorn
Haber Jennings
Robert Thorn
Carl Bugenhagen
Michael Morgan
Joan Hart
Bill Atherton
David Pasarian
Dr. William Kane
Mark Thorn
Charles Warren
Richard Thorn
Ann Thorn
Andrew Doyle
Brothers Benito
       Matteus
       Martin
       Paulo
       Antonio
       Simeon
Harvey Dean
Peter Reynolds
Kate Reynolds
Nurse Mary Lamont

Carol Wyatt
Father Thomas Doolan
Michael Finn
James Graham
Philip Brennan

May they all rest in peace.

And in memory of the author of their destruction, Damien Thorn, 1950-1982: may his soul writhe in torment for eternity. Remembered this day in the year of our Lord two thousand and one. London, England.

❧ Prologue ❧

FOR THREE DAYS the old man had lain almost motionless on his narrow bed, staring at the ceiling, oblivious to the competing blare of his bedside radio and the television in the corner.

He was dressed for work: tailcoat and pinstriped trousers, black shoes gleaming, the bow tie tight around the wax collar.

He was bald, his face podgy and pink and wet with tears. The room was a fetid fog of his own making, for he had soiled himself on the first night.

The newsreaders talked of only one thing, day and night. The war that everyone had named Armageddon had returned the Middle East to the desert; Tel Aviv and Jerusalem bombed to oblivion, Damascus and Beirut obliterated in retaliation.

The television showed the survivors in their refugee camps, then flashed satellite pictures of the radiation clouds drifting west with a forecast from meteorologists that the climate would change radically because of damage to the ionosphere.

None of this penetrated the old man's brain. Only the steady drip of tears from his chin onto the collar gave any indication that he was alive.

On the third night, the clouds cleared and moonlight speared a chink in the curtains. The old man blinked and sat up, swung himself off the bed, and made for the bathroom. All his life he had been a tidy man, and he knew what he had to do.

He washed and shaved, changed into an identical suit, dragged an overnight bag from his wardrobe, and made his way along the corridor to the staircase and down through the entrance hall, stopping briefly in the dining room to glance at the remains of a meal. Six candles had burned themselves out and black wax had made tracks across the mahogany. He grimaced in disgust and moved to the French windows. The mess would have to wait. There were more important things to be done.

It was a warm summer's night, but he shivered as he crossed the lawn to the stables, where he picked up a spade before slowly making his way up the hill toward the ruined church.

There were no more tears left in him now. He was a desert of grief. All his adult life he had believed in the force of evil and he had rejoiced in his faith. He had been promised eternal damnation, and he had welcomed the prospect. Now, since the carnage of that night, his soul had no future.

From the village came the sound of church bells, and he moved faster, cursing them. He had failed. All the disciples had failed, and there was no spirit left in any of them.

He was panting by the time he reached the church, and for a moment he leaned against the signpost that read *The Parish Church of St. John.* He gazed around him, knowing what he would see and hoping he would not go into shock again as he had three nights ago.

The dog lay where it had fallen, a massive beast, its black coat overlaid with dried blood and its yellow eyes staring sightlessly. It was lying at the feet of a crucifix that leaned against the church wall, a life-size effigy of Christ, nailed face on to the cross, the legs wrapped around the upright, arms stretched along the crossbeam. Like the dog, the face and torso were speckled with dried blood.

The old man put down the spade, stepped over the corpse, and slowly made his way into the church. All his life he had been too afraid to tread upon hallowed ground, but now that the war had been lost, there was no more fear, nothing against which to fight.

The church had neither roof nor pews, just a stone altar and a pulpit. The old man scuttled along the nave, trailing his bag, and stopped before the altar. The skeleton of a man lay in disarray with seven daggers scattered among the bones. He reached out for the skull, his fingers fluttering, then grabbed it, closed his eyes, and stuffed it into the bag, thinking it was all so undignified. He should have brought some kind of casket to carry away the mortal remains of Damien Thorn, but he had only the bag pasted with gaudy airline stickers.

In less than a minute he had completed the job, but the thighbones stuck out through the partially open zipper. The old man swore softly, then began collecting the daggers. They were identical; six inches of triangular steel blade, hilts fashioned in the shape of a crucifix with the body of Christ wrapped around them.

He stuffed the daggers into the bag, blew dust off the altar, then turned and moved as fast as he was able down the aisle. He was glad to leave the place; now there was just the burial and the burning.

It took him an hour to dig a grave big enough for the beast and another twenty minutes to gather gorse and twigs to stack around the base of the cross. When he was ready, he reached into his jacket and pulled out a lighter. At first the twigs would not light. The night wind kept blowing out the flame, but eventually the gorse began to smolder and he stepped back.

It was a tiny act of defiance, but there was nothing else.

That done, he bent to the dog, closed its eyes with his thumbs, then dragged it by its front paws to the edge of the grave. It weighed a hundred and fifty pounds, and the old man's heart lurched as he struggled with it, thinking that it would be ironic if the beast were to be the death of him. As he glanced at the grave, he thought that he might as well be digging it for himself.

In one final effort he bent and pushed at the rib cage, then stepped back as he felt a tremor in the body. He blinked and held onto the smoldering cross for support, staring at the corpse as it began to convulse, the hind legs kicking.

Without thinking what he was doing, the old man reached into the bag for one of the daggers, then knelt by the body and drew the knife across the belly. There was no blood; it was like cutting a tough steak. Again he moved back, stumbling in his fear as the creature's head emerged, blindly thrashing its way out of the torn womb. Its paws scrabbled for a grip, then it slithered over the ribs onto the newly dug soil, where it lay blind and motionless for a moment. Then it turned and began to gnaw at the umbilical cord.

The old man backed away, the pink glow of exertion on his face turning to gray.

"In the midst of death there is life," he muttered, then instinctively made the reverse sign of the cross as he felt his back becoming scorched.

He looked around into the face of the Christ effigy, the features obscured by smoke, then turned again as the first flash of lightning illuminated the grave, the pup gnawing at its freedom.

Then he was gone, moving as fast as his old legs would take him as the first drops of rain put out the fire, running blind so that he did not see two eyes in the woods watching him, pale yellow eyes, dull and lifeless.

The boy squatted in the bushes, oblivious to the downpour. He was naked. His hair was lank, his hands and feet filthy. Blood seeped from a cluster of wounds on his neck and ran, diluted by the rain, down his back. He sniffed the air as the smoke from the dying fire around the cross drifted toward him, then narrowed his eyes, focusing on the movement by the grave.

Slowly he began to crawl toward it, the tip of his tongue poking between his teeth. For a moment he stared at the pup, then leaned forward and began to lick it clean. The pup nuzzled him, then started scratching in the wet soil with its front paws, making lines and crosses. That done, it trotted toward the church, stopping every few feet to turn its head back in the boy's direction, urging him to follow.

At first the boy did not move, then he crawled up the path, whimpering. The hairs on his neck bristled, and goose pimples formed on his arms and legs. Briefly he stopped at the door, then crawled inside, following the pup to the pulpit. He looked up and bared his teeth in a snarl at the massive Bible, then looked down again at the pup. It was scratching again in the dust, identical markings:

XXII-III-VIII

Then the pup was running up the stone steps and sitting beside the lectern.

The boy touched the wounds on his neck and followed it, still at a crawl. When he reached the pulpit, he pulled himself to a half-crouch and sniffed the massive Bible. It was a New Testament, ancient and thick, covered by a shroud of dust.

He reached for it, fingers trembling, and opened it at the index, glanced at the books listed in Roman numerals. He did not need to translate. The message was there for him.

He turned to the twenty-second book and searched for the verse, his fingers leaving a trail of blood on the crumbling parchment. His finger stopped and he read slowly, lips moving silently, then he smiled and, for the first time, stood to his full height.

His eyes brightened and he clenched his fists in a gesture of triumph, then stiffened and looked around him, conscious of his nakedness and aware of his surroundings. He had permitted the ruined church to be left standing as a reminder of the impotence of Christianity; it was a ruin, but nonetheless it was still the house of God, and now the fear began to build in him, and he rejoiced. For if there was fear, then he was alive again, his spirit reborn.

He turned and ran, feeling the soles of his feet burn on the hallowed ground, and he reveled in his pain. Once outside, he stood looking at the crucifix, then turned to the old man's bag and drew out the seven daggers.

For a moment he stood in silent prayer, then he ran behind the crucifix and struck out, driving the first dagger into the spine and twisting it until the wood creaked. The rest of the task took him only a minute and then he stood back, nodding in satisfaction. Five daggers had been driven to their hilts at equal distance down the spine from the neck to the buttocks, the other two on either side in the shape of a cross.

Smiling, he moved to the front of the cross and stared at the agonized face, at the rivulets of rain running between the splashes of dried blood. When he spoke, his voice was corrupt with victorious contempt.

"As one day, Nazarene," he said. "A thousand years as one day." Then he was off, running down the slope toward the house as the downpour increased, and the eye sockets of Christ filled with rainwater and ran as tears down His face.

PART ONE

✌§ CHAPTER 1 §✍

PAUL BUHER HAD been waiting for death for nearly a year, and he was running out of patience. On the morning after the battle called Armageddon, he had had a minor stroke that had left his speech slightly impaired and a deadness in his left arm. He wished he had died of it because his life had been a blasphemy, a waste of seventy-one years, redeemed only at the end when he had turned away from evil and found Christ.

Now he was tired. In his last days he had forsworn luxury and moved into a cramped bedsitter in West London to wait out the winter, but there was to be no respite from the cold. Four days after the battle, in the middle of July in the year 2000, the first snow fell, and ever since, the land had remained under a thick layer of clouds.

There was neither autumn nor spring. Now, in June, the temperature was four degrees centigrade with a strong wind-chill factor. Daffodils and crocuses waited in vain to appear. The trees had been dead for almost a year, and the people walked hunched in the streets. They had been told often enough what had happened—the war had ruined the climatic balance—but knowing the reason did not make it any better.

That morning Buher sat sipping brandy. He could get through a bottle and a half a day now without any physical effect. The drink made him morbid and he could do without that, yet he could not give it up.

Slowly he got off the bed and switched on the television, glancing at the prophecies he had nailed to the wall. They all came from the Bible. He had taken verses, blown them up to the limit, and framed them.

Above his bed, in a frame four feet square, were the words: "And when ye shall see Jerusalem compassed with armies, then know that the desolation thereof is nigh. For these be the days of vengeance when all that is written shall be fulfilled."

Then, next to a newspaper photograph of the victims of the Damascus bombing, another quotation: "The people who have made war, their flesh will fall in rottenness. Their eyes will rot in their sockets, their tongues will rot in their mouths."

Above the door, so that he had to see it every time he left the room, was another:

"Let He who hath understanding
Reckon the number of the Beast;
For it is a human number,
Its number is Six Hundred and Sixty-six."

Each time he saw it, he touched the little scar on the index finger of his right hand. At first sight it seemed no more than a blemish of hard skin, three little circles, tadpoles of skin, each in the shape of a six. He had been proud when it appeared the day he had been initiated, but now he couldn't get rid of the damned thing, and if he found himself in company, he held his thumb over it to hide it.

Yet again, the newspapers had been full of pundits, still theorizing, a year after the event, trying to discover why the battle had ended so suddenly and why the war plans had not followed their inevitable course on that dreadful night.

Paul Buher knew the reason, but there was no one he could tell. Who, except for the fundamentalist fantatics, would believe that the Book of Revelation had foretold everything? That, following the Jews' return to Zion, Christ would walk the land again until he met his Antichrist at Armageddon?

The brandy bottle was tipped once more, and

Buher tried to concentrate on the midday news. It was a familiar litany of disaster. China and the Confederation of Nonaligned States had rejected the U.S.-Russian call for an arms freeze. The Chinese army was converging on the Russian border. The Security Council of the United Nations, called into emergency session, had condemned the latest border skirmishes and had called for the Chinese to pull back. As usual, it had been ignored.

Buher sighed and sipped. It was the old game of global paranoia. The names had been changed, but the possibility of another dreadful conflict was on the lips of every commentator, the scenario described so often that it seemed inevitable.

International anarchy was punctuated by acts of savagery at home. Rape competed with robbery for newstime, murder with arson. That morning there had been a particularly savage attack on an old people's home in Surrey, thirteen crippled men and women severely beaten, battered into unconsciousness, for their pensions.

Buher could take no more. He snapped off the set and glanced at the far wall. The largest biblical quotation of all dominated the room. For the hundredth time, Buher read aloud:

"And I saw an angel come down from heaven, having the key of the bottomless pit and a great chain in his hand. And he laid hold on the dragon, that old serpent, which is the Devil, and Satan, and bound him a thousand years, and cast him into the bottomless pit, and shut him up, and set a seal upon him, that he should deceive the nations no more, till the thousand years should be fulfilled: and after that he must be loosed a little season."

A thousand years. After Armageddon, the Millennium. That was the prophecy and the promise, but the promise had been phony, a dreadful betrayal.

Throughout the world, pessimism was rife. The war had stunned people into apathy. A pregnant woman was no longer congratulated on her conception; in the lands polluted by radiation, they waited to see the result, and even where there was safety, there was no joy in childbirth.

The human race waited quietly for extinction, and most thought it was deserved.

Buher glanced at his watch and reached for the phone. It was time for his daily check on Margaret to make sure she was all right.

He dialed and waited. No reply. He must have misdialed. He tried again; still nothing. Buher frowned. She should be in, or if not, someone should be there to look after the house—the nurse or the housekeeper. Quickly he reached for his coat and struggled into it, left the room, and hurried down the stairs, gagging at the stench of urine in the hallway. It was a dreadful slum to live in, but in a perverse way he enjoyed the deprivation. It was a sort of penance, like the stroke, an interlude of punishment before he died, before what he prayed would be an eternity of peace.

The cab took him two miles into South Kensington and Margaret Brennan's flat near the Boltons. There was no need for her to seek poverty; she had enough to cope with. Since that terrible night they had met every day. They needed one another, for there was no one else who would understand; but hers was the greater need because hers was the greater guilt.

His anxiety was tinged with panic as he got out of the cab and saw the policeman at the door. He gave his name, and the young man spoke into his radio, then stood back to let him in. All he would say was that there had been an accident.

The door to the flat was open, and Buher stood for a moment in the doorway. He had been there the previous morning, comforting her during one of her sobbing fits. The place had been untidy but now it was perfection. The windows sparkled, and there was a smell of furniture polish. Everything was in place. The only thing out of the ordinary was the two men in overcoats who looked at him expectantly.

The introductions were quickly made. A detective sergeant and his constable, both wearing similar expressions, somber and curious.

"Where is she?" Buher asked.

They told him the name of the hospital, and he frowned. "But that's . . ."

"Mental, sir, yes," said the sergeant.

Buher allowed himself to be led toward the bathroom, vaguely registering the policeman's warning that he should prepare himself. He stopped at the bathroom door and looked in. The white bath was striped with blood. It did not seem possible that there could be so much in one small woman.

Buher felt his legs buckle, and the policeman's hand on his weak arm. He turned to him, his eyes questioning.

"It would seem to have been an attempted abortion," the sergeant said, enunciating carefully as if by being formal, he would somehow lessen the horror of it. "Except that we're assured there was no fetus. The ambulance attendant said she was raving. Some lunacy about the spawn of the devil or some such thing.—" He shrugged apologetically, ashamed to be the bearer of such nonsense.

Buher closed his eyes, fighting the nausea. When he opened them, he found himself staring at an object in a plastic bag, a present he had given her years ago. It was a gold swizzle stick on a chain, worn as a necklace, something of a gimmick. It was their little joke and they had laughed, but she wore it occasionally when she was in that sort of mood.

It was six inches long when closed, but it was

open in the bag, the six spokes protruding and defiled by her blood.

"And just to be certain," the policeman was saying, "she had soaked the thing in bleach."

Again Buher felt his legs go, and he had to steady himself against the wall.

"Ingenious, don't you think, sir?"

"The poor woman." Buher stumbled over the words, his mind going off at a tangent. The policeman had probably made the normal assessment of him, thinking the slurred words were those of a drunk. Not that it mattered.

Now the sergeant was asking him if he knew of any reason why she should have done such a thing. Buher shook his head. If he tried to explain, to tell the truth, then the man's suspicions would be confirmed—drunk, or mad, or both.

"Can I see her?"

"Not yet, sir. There are questions to be asked, as soon as she's able."

Buher nodded, took one last look at the mess in the bathroom, and turned away, a wreck of a man, trying to control his nausea and dizziness but knowing he could never control his guilt.

⋲§ CHAPTER 2 §⋺

THE ANNOUNCEMENT FROM the headquarters of the Thorn Corporation in Chicago flashed around the world in the blink of a telex and set phones ringing in every major city. It was a short, simple statement: The seventeen-year-old son of Damien Thorn had, according to the will of his father, taken on his name and the chairmanship of the Thorn Corporation, and William Jeffries had become vice-president of the Thorn operation worldwide.

In every newsroom in the Western world, hastily convened conferences were called and the same questions asked. Who on earth was this young man? Who was his mother? Where had he been for the past seventeen years? When's the press conference? Where could they get a goddam picture?

It took a few hours for Buher to get the news. He had been drunk for three days since his last visit to Margaret Brennan's flat, pouring booze down himself to anesthetize body and mind. But as soon as he heard it, he sobered up. He stared in disbelief at the TV screen, clutching the armchair to stop the trembling in his arms.

He could see his reflection in the screen. His face had gone gray as his mind tried to assimilate the news. The picture flitted from the Thorn Headquarters in Chicago to Thorn UK on London's South Bank, to the gates of the old family residence in Chicago and on to the stately home in Berkshire called Pereford. Each scene was identical, with film crews and newspaper reporters impotently and impatiently waiting for answers to their questions.

Buher knew they would get none. The Thorn Corporation was accountable to no one. It was not a public company. There were no shareholders. Outsiders could only guess at the size of its turnover, and then even the wildest calculations were billions of dollars off.

Buher closed his eyes, knowing that the TV pictures in front of him had no relevance. He had failed. On that night they called Armageddon, he had not done enough. Like others before him, he thought he had succeeded, but the Beast would not die. The nightmare continued, and his bravery had been in vain.

Suddenly Buher did something he had not

done since he was a boy. He sobbed, long and loud, until his body hurt, but he did not care. Nothing mattered any more except seeing the boy again. It would be the last thing he did, but he could not die—either in peace or in torment— without that confrontation.

In the cab taking him out of London on the M4 toward Berkshire, Buher thought back to the time he had once considered to be the good old days, before his conversion to Christ, when the future seemed to hold a perverse promise.

Damien Thorn was going to control the world and the souls of mankind. It had been a time of energy and unlimited success. They had seemed immortal. The Thorn Corporation, in one generation, had become the biggest single industrial giant in the world, controlling the production and distribution of fertilizer and foodstuffs to the Third World. Its influence was felt in every political capital; everyone who was anyone owed the corporation something. There seemed to be no stopping them until that dreadful night when a woman named Kate Reynolds, whom Damien had taken as a lover, turned on him and drove a dagger into his spine.

Even after that, there was still hope. The woman bore a son, dying as she gave birth, and the child grew to be the image of his father and the custodian of his spirit.

Buher had watched him develop and at first

had taken care of him, but where Damien was charming, the son was gross, and where Damien wanted power and control, the son was interested in vengeance and destruction; and on the night of Armageddon, he had almost achieved it.

As the cab turned off the motorway and weaved through the country lanes toward Pereford, Buher began to tremble. He knew he was no match, physically or mentally, for the young man, but he needed to see him, to confront the object of his failure. If only he had taken his mission to its logical conclusion that night, then there would have been no need for this, but he had thought he had done enough.

Slowly he reached with his good right hand for his left and drew it to his face, holding his palms together, fingers clasped in the position of prayer. He began to murmur the words he had been taught as an infant, praying to his God for strength to see him through. The driver, glancing in his mirror, saw him praying and shrugged his shoulders. Another crazy man, he thought. What was there to pray for?

The security guard at the lodge gate had had a bad day. He had never seen such a rabble, all claiming to represent some newspaper or television station, all trying to get past him, pleading with him and cursing him in turn, talking among themselves; nervous people moving in circles, staring up the drive toward the house, giving off an almost visible current of tension. He was reminded of a pack of hounds milling around before the hunt.

For the hundredth time he told one of them that there would be no comment from the house, that they should transfer their attention to the main office in London. The reporter swore beneath his breath, and the guard watched him carefully, wondering if they would try to rush him. They were edgy enough to do that, and he quite welcomed the idea, for then he could call out the dogs.

As the black cab approached, the crowd turned and watched. Cameras were hoisted onto shoulders and notebooks fluttered. It stopped at the gate, and at first the guard could not see the passenger for the mob around it. Then it eased forward to him, and he looked in and blinked.

Paul Buher had aged ten years since he had last seen him. Where before he had been tall and straight, now he was stooped and thin, a wreck of a man. But it was Buher, all right, and the guard felt a tremor of uncertainty. His was a simple life, and he had a straightforward set of rules. For twenty years he had been saluting Mr. Buher, standing back to let him pass, acknowledging him as the top man. Then there had been a new instruction. Now Paul Buher was just another outsider.

The guard pushed through the crowd, ignoring their questions. A year ago they would not have needed to ask who Buher was. Now the change in him made him anonymous.

He bent low as Buher wound the window down. Microphones were pushed in, but Buher ignored them.

"Is he in?"

There was only one "he."

"Yes sir." The "sir" was said automatically.

"Call him, will you? Tell him I'm here."

The guard was relieved. At least Mr. Buher had spared him the responsibility of refusing him admission. He went into the lodge and spoke into the house phone, then nodded, came out again, and helped the old man out of the cab. He would have to walk. If the gates were opened to let the taxi through, the reporters would follow.

The cameras whirred and the reporters yelled questions as he helped Buher to the lodge.

"You know where to go, sir," he said, closing the door behind him.

Buher nodded, went out the back door, and shuffled slowly up the drive. Watching him, the guard wondered if he would make it. He had never seen a man so ill and so nervous. . . .

Buher had never walked the length of the drive. He had always been in limousines, his mind preoccupied with business. Now the drive seemed to stretch and bend forever, and when he made the final turn and saw the house, he felt afraid. With death so close, he suddenly did not want it. It was one thing to pass away peacefully, quite another to face whatever fate the boy had in mind for him.

He looked around. The rose garden was dead. There was not a leaf on the trees. Even the great house looked shabby. Pereford should have been a joy, one of the country's stateliest homes; sixty-three rooms, three hundred and fifty years old, a magnificent place set on four hundred acres, but corrupted by the abomination that now inhabited it.

The front door was open, and he stepped into the entrance hall, standing motionless for a moment, sniffing like a dog. There was no sense of ownership, no smell of cooking or of polish. It was a dead place. He had never entered without being welcomed by George the butler, that old man with the pink face who was always anxious to please.

Buher called out for him, but his voice echoed, a shrill, thin voice, weak with age. Slowly he mounted the great staircase, thinking back to the last time he had been here when the boy had carried that strange crucifix down the stairs. He remembered it slipping on his shoulder, the crown of thorns piercing the boy's neck and drawing blood.

He shivered as he reached the bedroom, pushed the door open, and looked inside. It was exactly as he remembered it, painted maroon, the narrow, celibate bed flanked by a portrait of the boy's father and a photograph of the grave of his mother.

The collage of photographs had gone, the Warsaw ghetto, the devastation of Hiroshima and Dresden, on which the boy had scrawled the word REHEARSALS. With a shudder of recognition Buher saw that it had been replaced by a photograph of himself, covered with incomprehensible scrawls.

Gently he closed the door and moved along the corridor. He knew where the boy would be, in the black room at the end, the place he called his chapel. Buher only hoped that he would have the nerve to go in.

When he first saw it, he thought it was the same dog, but as he gazed into the eyes, only six feet away, he saw that the markings were slightly different. This was a bigger, younger animal. It was the size of a deer, and it was growling at him.

Buher backed off. Above the noise of the beast he could hear a familiar litany through the black door, and he knew the boy was in there, praying, drawing strength again. He knew that he could not go in. As he turned and moved quickly back the way he had come, he cursed his conceit of the past twelve months, his arrogant belief that it was possible to conquer evil. It was such a preposterous piece of optimism.

There was only one thing left for him to do.

He had to try to find the daggers—not that he would have the strength to use them, but if he could keep them safe, then perhaps someone younger and stronger could finish the job.

Slowly he made his way back down the stairs and out onto the lawn, his feet crunching on the frosted grass. Heading up the hill toward the church, he felt like a pilgrim on his last journey.

The crucifix was propped against the church wall, and from a distance, he did not realize what was different about it. Then he saw that the legs had been burned away, almost to the loincloth.

When he reached the spot, he got down on his knees in prayer and gazed into the wooden face of Christ. The nails that represented the crown of thorns had rusted, and frost sparkled in the eyesockets. Over the shoulder, Buher could see the hilts of the daggers, and he got to his feet and gave thanks. The Lord had guided him and shown him the way. He went to the back of the crucifix and gazed at the desecration of the body. There was only one creature who could have done this, who knew the significance of the sequence. The daggers had to be planted in the shape of the cross; otherwise they were useless.

He touched each one of them. Like the crown of thorns, the hilts had rusted so that the seven faces of Christ were unrecognizable, but he had found them, and that was all that mattered.

He reached for the nearest and tugged. It did

not move. He tried both hands, the weak left hand underneath the strong right hand for support. Again he pulled. Nothing. He placed one foot on the shoulder of the figure and heaved. Sweat pumped from his forehead, but the dagger did not budge.

He could not do it. He was too frail.

Slowly, trying to draw breath, he made his way into the church to pray once more for guidance. He stopped at the altar and ran his hand along the dust, then looked up at the pulpit and saw the Bible. Painfully he climbed the steps and looked at it. The book was open, a bloodstain marking a verse. He checked it; the Second Epistle General of Peter, in the New Testament chapter three, verse eight.

He read it without thinking:

"But, beloved, be not ignorant of this one thing, that one day is with the Lord as a thousand years, and a thousand years as one day."

At first he did not understand; for a few seconds he frowned in confusion, until he remembered the quote in his room, about the devil's being locked away for a thousand years. The Millennium. As one day.

He felt his heart shudder and a pain run down his left arm, and when he spoke again, his speech was slurred, a distorted cry of anguish. It was a false prophecy. Time had no meaning. There could be no peace.

He made his way out of the church. There was one task left for him. If he could not get the daggers, at least he could make them safe. He went back for the crucifix and dragged it by the head along the path and into the church, knowing that the boy would not dare step onto hallowed ground. He rested it against the altar and looked up through the shattered roof at the heavy snowclouds and was not satisfied. Maybe the boy would send his disciples, those obscene jackals, to search for it. He could take no chances.

For a full minute he looked at the one remaining beam, the great two-foot-thick joist that ran twenty feet above, between the crumbling walls.

He knew where there was a ladder and strong rope, and he prayed that he would have the strength to do the job.

An hour later he was finished. The crucifix gazed down at him, roped to the beam, and Buher smiled up at it.

"A resurrection," he said, then turned and walked out of the church.

As he made his way past the house, he stopped and looked up. At a window he could see the boy looking down at him. Briefly they stared at one another, then Buher turned and made his way back down the drive. He knew the boy would not harm him. There was no point. The boy would know what was in his mind.

*   *   *

Back in the sanctuary of his room, Buher prayed on his knees for ten minutes, then painfully got to his feet and took a small tape recorder from the shelf, poured himself a brandy, and settled back to make his confession.

"Father, forgive the way I speak," he said into the machine. "It is the result of a stroke, but I pray you will bear with me and try to understand."

He played the sentence back and nodded in satisfaction. The words were clear enough. His final message would get through.

"My name is Buher," he continued. "We have never met, but I am well aware of the power of your faith and I pray to God that you are still with us. If not, then I entrust this confession to your successor in the hope that he will receive it. I know that this will sound strange, this disembodied voice talking to you in a foreign tongue, but there is no one else, no one I can trust."

He paused, reached for his Bible and held it on his lap, then bent once more to the machine.

"Father, forgive me for a lifetime of sin. . . ."

It took him two hours to make the tapes. When he was done, he sealed them in a padded bag and addressed it: Father De Carlo, Monastery of San Benedetto, Subiaco, Italy. Then he dragged on his coat and left for the post office. He knew the package would get there too late and he

40

could only hope that forgiveness could be post-dated, that redemption could be posthumous.

Once he had gotten rid of it, he felt relieved. He had made his confession. The rest was up to his God.

A strong wind blew as he left the building. It was only a few hundred yards to the house, but he had to fight for every step, head down against the gale. A passerby looked twice at him, wondering why he was smiling, what was wrong with the crazy man. And what was he saying to himself?

Buher's words were lost in the wind. "The Antichrist has the power over men's minds." He repeated it like litany, all the way to his flat.

At first the main door wouldn't open. He dragged at it, pulling against the wind that held it shut. He knew that if he turned, he would be confronted by some vision. He knew that he was under attack, knew of others who had been destroyed by the demonic power that corrupted the mind like a mental cancer from within. The boy was playing with him, enjoying a last, perverse joke.

Finally he was through into the hall, slamming the door behind him. Briefly he leaned against it, feeling the wind zip through the letter box, making it clatter, then he moved up the stairs, clutching the banister, fighting for breath.

In his room he settled himself on the bed. The brandy and the pills were close at hand. It was time. He reached for them. He was taking far too long to die. The spirit was weak, but the flesh was surprisingly strong. He would have to do something about it.

He could only pray that the Lord would understand. He was counting on that one thing for salvation, that this act of speeding up his death was not considered a sin and would not exclude him from His Kingdom.

There was a notepad and a pen on the bedside table. He reached for them and began to write one sentence that summed up his life:

WHAT DOES IT PROFIT A MAN, IF HE SHALL GAIN THE WHOLE WORLD, AND LOSE HIS OWN SOUL?

As he dropped the pen, he glanced at the index finger of his right hand. The mark was still there. Paul Buher sighed and picked up the brandy bottle.

"Amen," he said.

❧ PART TWO ❧

⇜§ CHAPTER 3 §⇝

THE DEATH OF Paul Buher made front-page news in the *New York Times* with a lengthy obituary on page two. The writer did not feel the need to bother with the rule of not speaking ill of the dead, describing Buher as a ruthless enigma who trampled people to get to the top.

It was grudgingly admitted that it was Buher's foresight that had made the Thorn Corporation the biggest of the industrial giants, that it was he who had taken Thorn into fertilizer and soya. It was he who had seen that the control of foodstuffs would reap huge financial and political dividends, and Buher's most famous line was quoted:

"Our porfitable future lies in famine."

Then the writer added sourly that Buher, in

common with the rest of the Thorn people, had never given an interview and consequently very little was known about him or his views.

And there was a hint of gloating in the description of his death in poverty in a "seedy" apartment, a year after resigning from the best-paid and most powerful job in the Western business world. The obituary finished on a note of coincidence, that the man had died soon after the announcement of the young Damien Thorn's taking over the corporation.

It was this final point that stuck in the mind of Jack Mason as he put the paper down and stared out through the fog that rose from the East River. Mason lived thirty stories above midtown Manhattan, in an apartment that cost him ten thousand dollars a month. For a year, all he had seen was fog. One of the selling points of the place had been the glorious view across the river to Queens and as far as Long Island, but the war had put an end to that, and he cursed the warmongers as he had done every day for a year.

Mason went back to the paper and read the obituary again, conscious of the special excitement that occurred whenever an idea for a book was conceived.

Tucking the paper under his arm, he went into the small bedroom that he had turned into an office. One wall was taken up with the covers of the fifteen books he had written. The opposite wall, covered in cork tiles, was bare. Mason cut out the obituary and pinned it to the board, then stood back and looked at it. Soon, if the idea took shape, the wall would be covered with news clippings and notes about the Thorn Corporation.

Mason rubbed his hands and reached for the phone. . . .

Three hours later he was lunching with his agent. Mason had picked a small bar on the Lower East Side, a place where he wouldn't be recognized where no one would be interested in his conversation. Only Harry was going to be let in on the *idea* at this stage.

"You're crazy," Harry said.

"I knew you'd say that."

"No one's ever gotten near the Thorn Corporation." The little man squealed with indignation. He was a professional cynic who rejected every idea brought to him on the theory that if his writers could convince him, they could convince anyone. But this was different. This was a problem of massive proportions. It couldn't be done, and he told Mason so.

"Look," he said, trying to be patient, "once upon a time there were leaks from Hyannis Port about the Kennedys, then there was that lucky Khashoggi book. Okay, sometimes the Mafia gets leaked until they plug it. Even the English royal family gets leaked. But the Thorns?" He shrugged his shoulders. "Never."

"Which is why I'm going to do it," said Mason patiently.

Harry looked up at his client. He had to. Everybody looked up at Mason. He was six-three and weighed two hundred pounds excluding the beard. Fifty years old, he did everything to excess. Someone had once written that he made Hemingway seem effeminate. Journalists could never resist the cliché "larger than life," and even those who disapproved of his behavior could not deny that he was far and away the best writer of his generation.

Harry snuffled into his mineral water and tried something he knew was impossible. Jack Mason had never been dissuaded, not once an idea had impregnated his brain, but he had to try. He was still trying six hours later in P. J. Clarke's on Third Avenue and trying to remember to talk in code in case any literary groupies were listening. The latest Mason book was news, and it was far too early for that, maybe two years too early.

"Jack, you've got two Pulitzers," Harry was saying.

"Sure, and three ex-wives with charge cards."

"So do another epic."

Mason raised his hands, big as shovels, and for a moment Harry thought he was about to be throttled. "Just listen for a moment. I told you this before. I'll tell you again. This morning I got hold of the newspaper cuttings on the Thorns, and I haven't had time to read them properly but what shines through is that everyone who comes into contact with them—"

"I know, I know," said Harry impatiently. "You told me already. They come to sticky ends."

"Philip Brennan," said Mason, raising one finger and pointing it between Harry's eyes. "Just one case. U.S. Ambassador to the Court of St. James's. Where does he go on his last night?"

"How should I—"

"Pereford. The Thorn country estate. Why does he go there? What's the connection?"

"Who knows?"

"Right. Ten days later his body is found. Stabbed in the throat, teeth marks on his shoulder. At his cremation his wife throws herself on the goddam coffin as it goes through the gates and gets second-degree burns."

"So?"

"It's a story, that's so."

"So leave it to the journalists."

"Journalists hell. I wanna do them bastard Thorns."

"You'll never reach page one."

It was the wrong thing to say, and Harry knew it even as the words tumbled out of his treacherous mouth. Again he thought that Mason was going to choke him.

"Fictionalize it," he tried, knowing it was a

blunder when Mason shook his head. The big man had had enough. He hadn't convinced the agent and he'd had enough booze not to care. On the way out he knocked over two bar stools—occupied bar stools, but no one complained. It was just Jack.

Harry watched him walk out in anger and a cloud of enthusiasm into the fog; a month, he reckoned, maybe two, then he'd come to his senses. . . .

Mason got no sleep that night. The pile of newspaper cuttings from his friend on the *Times* took a lot of reading, and the more he read, the more convinced he was that this was the story of the century. The disasters that befell the Thorns and everyone around them made the Kennedys look lucky.

The story had everything: graft and corruption, a jinxlike virus, and now this strange kid who appeared from nowhere and claimed to be the son of Damien Thorn. The boy must be an impostor, but how to prove it?

The news of Buher's death did not reach the monastery in Subiaco. There was no television and no newspaper. It was an ancient place, a vast stone building dating from the twelfth century, sixty miles and five hundred years away from Rome.

That morning, as was his custom, the young

monk named Francis visited the grave of his priest. A small headstone marked the spot.

Antonio De Carlo
1920–2000 A.D.

It was a peaceful resting place in a copse next to the vineyard, the old man laid to rest alongside his predecessors.

Dressed in sandals and a brown cassock, the young man stood by the grave, head bowed, murmuring a prayer and thinking, as he did each day, of the blessed, merciful ignorance that had marked the old man's last moments.

He had died the day after the war everyone called Armageddon. It was the one time a radio had been permitted in the monastery, and together the priest and the monk listened to the news, to the astonishment of the pundits relating the signing of SALT 4 between the Russians and the Americans and the statement that the terrible carnage in the Middle East had served a purpose. It had brought the world's leaders to their senses.

Francis remembered the smile on the old man's face and his final words before he died, that now there would be peace.

All his life Father De Carlo had fought the forces of evil. Once he thought he had won, and the knowledge that his triumph had turned to failure had almost killed him. A second failure would have been too much for him to bear, but the Lord, in his mercy, had spared him that. The final mercy, ignorance as bliss, a blessed relief. The old man had died with a smile on his face, and Francis had been at his side. There had been no pain. The deep creases in his face seemed to soften at the moment of death, and he had accepted it as a relief. His last words were a blessing and not a curse, and for that Francis gave daily thanks.

His vigil completed, he turned and made his way back to his room. He had already packed for the journey, just a small suitcase, since he had very few worldly possessions. The cassettes lying on top of his clothes looked incongruous, a reminder of the century that he inhabited, but to which he did not belong.

It had taken him two days to go to the town and borrow a tape recorder, and when he sat alone in his room listening to the confession of Paul Buher, he had burst into tears. It was not over after all. The nightmare had to be lived again, and Buher had shown the way.

Among the monks, Francis was the experienced one. He had taken the trip to London before, to face the power and the wrath of the Antichrist, and he thought he had succeeded in his mission. Father De Carlo had blessed him for his bravery, but it had not been enough.

Now, as he waited for the bus to take him to Rome, he wondered if he had the nerve to make a second attempt. He no longer had the spirit of the priest to support him. He had only his faith in Jesus Christ, and God knew, he thought, that should be more than enough; why, then, he wondered, was he so afraid?

At Rome airport he waited patiently at the check-in desk for his boarding pass. He had walked past the newsstand, ignored the newspapers. Had he stopped, he would have seen Paul Buher's face on the cover of *Time* magazine, but Brother Francis did not read newspapers or magazines, and an hour later he boarded his flight, blissfully ignorant that the man he was setting off to see had been buried three days earlier.

CHAPTER 4

THE FLEET OF limousines eased its way through the lodge gateway, illuminated by the flashlights of the cameras, each reporter ducking to see who was in the back, a chorus of questions going unanswered as the gate was finally shut.

The count had been six limos and a Rolls-Royce sports car, and a lot of guessing as to who had sat behind the smoked-glass windows. With nothing better to go on, the reporters interviewed each other, tried to get a check on the license plates, and finally came to a consensus that the Thorn Corporation board was in session.

The guesswork was inspired. The first man out was William Jeffries, formerly of the State Department and now chairman of the corporation, easing himself out of the Rolls to be greeted by George, the butler. The others followed in line, like ducklings, by order of importance, each man identically suited in black, and each one consumed with curiosity.

The old butler wheezed as he showed the men into the massive drawing room where a log fire blazed day and night throughout the summer, illuminating the life-size portrait of Damien Thorn that hung above the mantelpiece.

Jeffries stood beneath the painting and stared into the stern face of the man he had worshiped, feeling, as always, a sense of awe spiced with a pinch of jealousy. Thorn had been a handsome man, tall and dark in the classic, traditional mold, while Jeffries was thin and pale, with washed-out eyes and spare, graying hair. Occasionally it galled him that Damien should have had everything.

A voice at his elbow interrupted his thoughts, and he turned to see the old butler offering him a sherry and whispering that he was wanted upstairs.

Jeffries excused himself, glanced briefly at the others grouped stiffly and formally around the coffee table, and noticed with a smile that they had formed into a rectangle, taking up the positions they held at the boardroom table.

It took George an eternity to lead him up the staircase, stopping for breath every second step. Jeffries walked patiently behind him, listening to the wheezing and the rattling. The old man sounded like a broken-down lawnmower.

At the top George rested for a moment and gestured along the corridor toward the west wing.

"He wants you to witness this, sir," he said.

Then the old man set off, shuffling his feet. Jeffries followed, feeling the tension build in him. He had never seen the son of Damien Thorn. Only Buher had seen him. Buher had been the link man, Buher, who had betrayed him. And for what? Jeffries wondered as he often had. Even Judas had a motive and a reward, but for Buher there were no pieces of silver, just a needless death in poverty.

The corridor darkened as they reached a corner and turned left, and Jeffries smelled the beast before he saw it, heard the growl deep in the throat before he saw the yellow eyes. He had always been afraid of dogs, especially enormous creatures like the Rottweiler. Damien had always had them, and now the son was carrying on the tradition. Jeffries knew that his fear was irrational, because it was just a guard dog, and on his side. But the logical part of his brain was no match for the instinctive terror.

The dog got to its feet and was staring past George at him. Malevolent eyes, brutal teeth. Jeffries recalled something he had read, that if you grab the front legs and push outward as they leaped at you, then the heart would burst.

But it wouldn't be easy, not with your throat torn out.

He was aware of his own smell, the odor of fear. The dog's hackles rose and the growl deepened, but died immediately when the old man shushed it and patted the great head, then turned and smiled.

"I was the midwife," he said. "More or less."

Before Jeffries could take in the meaning, the door was pushed open and he was past the dog, standing inside the chapel. Buher had once described it to him, a black circular room, supported by six pillars with a stone altar in the center. What Jeffries had not expected was the smell. It was rank, like the slaughterhouse he had once visited when he was a kid in Chicago.

As his eyes grew accustomed to the dark, he could see that the floor was covered with what looked like dried blood, and the walls were splashed with it.

"I would not have it cleansed," said a voice to his left. He turned and saw the young man staring at him. He was dressed in a black cassock his feet bare. Jeffries nodded a greeting and looked into his eyes. They were dark and intense, but there was something strange about them, and he thought of the old clichés, the stoat with the rabbit, the cobra with the mongoose.

"After that night," he was saying, "I left the blood where it wa spilled. I would not have it cleansed."

Then the young man was leading him by the arm to the center of the room, and he could see a casket, three feet by two, on the altar, black with a satin cover.

"The mortal remains of my father," he said, and Jeffries suppressed a blasphemous giggle. It seemed incongruous somehow. Then he felt the grip tighten on his sleeve, felt himself forced to kneel. He turned and looked into the young man's face.

"I want you to witness this," he said quietly.

Jeffries blinked and shrank away from him. The young man pulled at the cowl of the cassock, exposing his neck. Blood seeped from seven puncture marks. He touched them with the fingers of his left hand.

"The stigmata of the Nazarene," he said, reaching out for him. Instinctively Jeffries drew back, then checked himself, afraid of causing offense.

"Taste the blood."

Jeffries could not do it. He wanted out of this terrible place, but his legs would not obey the orders from his brain. The fingers were almost at his lips now. Behind them the boy was staring at him.

"Taste it," he said again.

Still Jeffries held back.

"The priests of the Nazarene demand that His followers drink of his blood and eat of his flesh.

I demand less." The boy's fingers were on his lips "Just the blood," he said.

It was hot and scalded him, tasting sour, but Jeffries did as he was bid for there was no choice. Then it was over and he was looking into the boy's face. Again he touched the wounds, and this time the fingers were raised to Jeffries's forehead.

"I anoint you," he said, and again the blood scalded him. Jeffries felt the blood run down his face, and he reached up to wipe it away. When he looked at his fingers, they glistened. On his index finger he saw that a scab had formed, a tiny blemish in the shape of three sixes curling into one another.

He vaguely heard the boy's voice telling him that he had taken his father's name, but Jeffries could hardly register the fact. As he left the room he noticed that the dog no longer growled and the old man was smiling at him. As they made their way back along the corridor, Bill Jeffries felt defiled, and he gloried in the feeling.

The six men were still standing in the same positions, and Jeffries could sense their nervousness. To relax them he asked George to pass around the sherry. They talked among themselves, too loud, masking the tension.

Jeffries glanced from one to another, thinking how the balance of power had affected them. Those who had worked on the Middle East desk were long gone. The two men from Peking were now more important than either the Washington bureau chief or the man from NATO.

It was Russia and China now, the principal players. The West was little more than irrelevant.

The door opened, and they turned as one to see the young Damien Thorn framed in the doorway. He had changed into slacks and a shirt, and Jeffries noticed that the marks on his neck had vanished.

Jeffries as rehearsed, made the introductions. Each man shook Damien's hand, then stepped back, conscious of his gaze. Two of them, the Americans, had grumbled together about the meeting and had even talked openly about the possibility that Damien was an impostor. Now they both knew that their thoughts were heretical, and as flesh touched flesh, they knew something worse—that he knew what they had been thinking. And they could only hope for forgiveness.

George, wandering among them with his tray, saw the father in the son. There was no trace of the mother, none of Kate Reynolds' gentleness, no softness, no femininity. She had been no more than a vessel for the abominable seed, and even as he thought about her, he became aware that Damien was looking at him reproachfully. He had to move away, for he, more than any of the others, knew that there were no secrets.

The meeting lasted an hour, each man giving his report without interruption. When they finished, Damien asked his questions. Jeffries, listening intently, was impressed, recalling Buher's words that the boy, like his father, grasped detail quickly and had a memory like a computer. There was no humor, no small talk, just rapid, incisive questions.

When it was over, Damien looked up at the portrait of his father, then turned to the others.

"Gentlemen," he said, "I want to thank you for coming."

They nodded back at him, some smiling, others expressionless.

"However, I will not see any of you again. I have no intention of presenting myself to the public world. Bill Jeffries will continue to run the operation and will answer to me." He paused. "That is all."

They were dismissed and filed out silently in order of importance.

Jeffries stopped as he heard his name called and turned back. Damien was gesturing to him to stay behind, and for a fraction of a moment, Jeffries felt a tremor of annoyance that he should be taking orders from someone scarcely out of adolescence. But as quickly as the blasphemous thought rose, it vanished. He could taste the blood again, and it was like bile. He offered a silent apology and saw Damien smile, accepting it.

They walked together through the rose garden,

Damien plucking the dead flowers and crushing them, then ticking off points on his fingers.

"To sum up," he said, "we have finally put a stop to the one-child-family nonsense in China."

Jeffries nodded. "The annual population growth is now twenty million." He smiled. "In round figures, that is." But Damien did not smile back. There was no flippancy in him. Jeffries coughed to hide his embarrassment and continued, "Which means that they must expand their borders to survive."

"Like Hitler's Germany," said Damien.

"Exactly."

"And the date is set for the Taiwan invasion?"

Again Jeffries nodded. "Just a sideshow. A rehearsal for the push north."

"And the army?"

"With the latest recruitment figures, it should top five million by the end of the year."

"A plague of locusts," said Damien, smiling briefly for the first time. Then he gazed eastward. "And Tokyo?" he asked.

"No problem," replied Jeffries. "The yen is getting stronger daily, and the dollar is on the skids. The Republicans will soon release their official policy that the West can no longer shelter behind tariff barriers. It must compete."

"Conclusion?"

"The trade war becomes a shooting war."

"More Hiroshimas," said Damien.

"More Nagasakis," said Jeffries.

Again Damien smiled. "On two fronts, China and the nonaligned countries threatening Russia, the Japanese threatening the economy of the West, the Middle East oil pipeline shattered by the war. Iran and Iraq at each other's throats again." He spread his arms wide. "Global anarchy," he said happily.

Jeffries, looking at him, felt cold.

"A thousand years of peace," Damien said. "What a mockery."

There was just one question remaining, a minor point, but it was something Jeffries had read which bothered him.

"Have you heard about this book by the writer Mason?" he asked.

Damien nodded.

"Do you want me to do anything about him?"

"Why?"

"I thought maybe he might pose some kind of . . ." He searched for the word. Threat? Danger? But even as he hesitated, he saw Damien walk away, uninterested.

Jeffries shrugged his shoulders and scolded himself for stupidity. What had he been thinking of? What could a mere scribe do in the face of such power? Even a scribe with a million-dollar advance and two Pulitzers? Damien was right. The idea was absurd.

CHAPTER 5

THE FIRST DAYS were always the worst. The brain was riddled like Swiss cheese with doubt, there was fear that the idea was no good, panic that even if it was okay, then he wouldn't be able to write it, that the talent, or what passed for talent, had dried up. But at least this idea wasn't fiction. With fiction, he always had the realization that he was conning people. Who was going to be interested in the fantasies of a fifty-year-old anyway?

No, Mason thought, this was a good story. The only trouble was getting hold of it.

For three hours he had gone through a pile of newspaper cuttings. The earlier stuff was yellow and crumbled in his hand; the latest was new enough to stain his fingers with ink. But it all told the same story. The Thorns were jinxed. From Kathy Thorn, Damien's mother, who died in a fall from a hospital window, to Damien himself, a cardiac victim at the age of thirty-two, none had died peacefully in a bed or lasted the normal life span.

He yawned and stretched, stiff from hunching over his desk, and when he looked down again at the cuttings, the story of Philip Brennan was on the top of the pile.

He read it for the third time; the mystery of the body in the woods and the terrible wounds, said by the coroner to have been caused by a particularly nasty blade, six inches long and molded in a triangular shape so that any wound would never heal.

Not that Brennan's wound had had a chance to heal, not a six-inch wound in the jugular, but at least death would have been quick, if that was any consolation. Mason wasn't sure. You couldn't be sure if you did not know what was on the other side. What if it was agony for eternity? A soul in constant torment? What then? No one had ever come back to tell.

Then there were the marks on one hand and a shoulder, teeth marks of a larg dog, the inquest had been told, the distinctive jaw of a Rottweiler. Mason blinked. He didn't know one dog from another. What the hell was a Rottweiler, and why had it attacked the U.S. Ambassador to the

Court of St. James's somewhere in the Berkshire countryside?

Then there was the grisly sequel to the story when, at his cremation in London, Brennan's wife, Margaret, had thrown herself on the coffin as it was being trundled into the flames.

The story raised numerous questions, but the one that interested Mason the most was the statement from Brennan's secretary at the American embassy that he had been on his way to the Thorn country house to have dinner with Paul Buher on the night everyone now called Armageddon.

Mason smelled something odd. On the face of it, there was nothing wrong with Brennan's going to dine with Buher, but the history of the Thorn Corporation was a saga of potential corruption. That they had their men in positions of power and influence from Chicago to China, from Washington to Peking, Tokyo to Moscow, was well known and, on the face of it, quite acceptable. But Mason had worked on many a corruption story in his younger days. He believed, like an old English journalist he had once met, that the only way to deal with a politician was to assume that he was telling lies.

Mason was a professional cynic. Politics and business interest did not mix without the added ingredient of graft. The Thorn Corporation was the biggest, most powerful business machine on the planet, and as sure as hell, when their executives went calling on the politicians, it wasn't just for a friendly round of golf.

Philip Brennan should have been in London on the night the bombs fell in Jerusalem. He had been called to Downing Street like the other ambassadors in that moment of extreme crisis. He had no right to be wrestling with some damn dog in a country ditch.

As he pinned the cuttings to his wall and stood back to stare at them, Mason realized that a great chunk of the Thorn book would have to be researched in London. For that he needed help, and he knew the woman for the job.

Anna Brompton put everything on hold after the call from New York. She had three small projects she was working on, but nothing that couldn't be postponed or laid off on someone else. When Jack Mason called, you jumped to attention.

What he was attempting seemed at first glance—and even second glance—to be impossible, but she could easily suspend her misgivings. It was his responsibility, and if he thought it could be done, who was she to argue? She considered it a privilege to work with him. Besides, the job would be no small comfort to her bank manager.

She thought back. It must have been three years since they had met, and she had forgotten how excited she could get at the sound of his rough, staccato voice, always talking five minutes ago, unlike those in the sleepy publishing world that she moved in.

The next morning a sheaf of cuttings and a lengthy briefing letter arrive by express mail, and she wasted no time immersing herself in the story. The Philip Brennan angle seemed to be the one to go for first, and right away she got lucky.

Donna Elrod was now semiretired and lived in Kent. Anna had gotten her number from a friend in the U.S. embassy press department, but when she'd phoned, she had been apprehensive. Private secretaries were by definition, loyal creatures, secretive and tight-lipped when dealing with the affairs of the boss, even after the boss was dead. But Donna Elrod said she'd be pleased to talk.

Anna drove down that morning, and by lunchtime they were on their second bottle of wine in Donna's cottage. There was an immediate rapport. Anna liked the woman. Donna looked to be about fifty, with dark, hennaed hair. Her conversation was sharp, and she was eager to talk, as if by chattering about Philip Brennan she was soothing the pain of loss.

"He'd been acting very strange at the end," she said, "like going off to Rome for some reason. God knows why."

"Did he say where?"

Donna nodded. "A monastery somewhere. He

was going to see a priest. De Carlo, I think it was. Something like that."

Anna made notes.

"He was a strange man. Just before he died we were trying to think of somewhere he could go on holiday with his wife. He said there was nowhere a man of conscience could go anymore. Half the world treated human rights as a joke."

She smiled. "I remember what he said about the Arabs: "They have either gone fundamental or the other way."

"Huh?"

"That's what I said. Either gone back to the Middle Ages or gone all reflective glasses and automatic pistols." She laughed again, and Anna joined in.

"So," she continued, "I suggested Spain, but he rejected that because they'd gone fascist again. The Caribbean was out because the islands were run either by the mob or some half-assed dictator. The Indian Ocean had gone commie. I remember suggesting Sweden. 'Sweden,' he said. 'I'd need an armored truck in Sweden.' The kids there had just shot the Norwegian ambassador for being too right-wing."

Her smile faded, and she shook her head. "The world's in a mess, don't you think?"

Anna nodded in agreement, then tried to steer her in another direction, asking her if she had any idea why he had been murdered.

Donna shook her head. "If the police don't know, how could I?"

"Yes, well . . ."

"What a terrible way to die," she said softly. "Who could think up such thing as a triangular blade?" Her voice cracked and her lips trembled. "The human mind is perverted. Don't you think?" She looked up for support, and Anna again nodded in agreement. "It's time we gave the world over to the insects. Give them a chance."

Anna tried to change the mood. "I remember as a kid reading one of the news magazines. The whole thing was devoted to the possibility of insects taking over the world. Then in the next issue they carried a letter from some guy saying, 'If flies are so smart, how come they can't figure out window panes?'"

But Donna didn't laugh. "Radiation doesn't affect them, you know." she said. "Think how fat they're going to get on all the bodies."

It was time to go.

On the way back to London, Anna played the tape of the conversation. She hadn't gotten much except a good source. It was obvious that Donna had made the classic mistake and fallen in love with her boss. Now she was paying for it.

The invitation was to the tenth birthday party of a publishing company, a drinks-and-canapé affair at one of the classier Soho restaurants. Anna decided to go and give herself a few hours off. She'd been deep into the Thorn research for three days and was becoming depressed by her lack of success. She was beginning to wonder if this could be the first mistake Jack Mason had made in his long career.

Not that she expected to enjoy the publishing party much, all that standing around and mingling, getting heartburn from the cheap white wine, watching authors drinking greedily in lieu of royalties, observing the little flirtations and the managing directors pretending to be making deals with agents.

She never planned to enjoy them, but somehow she always wound up talking to someone she liked, and then there would be a meal somewhere and bed late with a head like vinegar next morning and maybe a few memory blanks. . . .

She checked herself in the mirror. Her hair was okay, a bit mousy maybe but nicely cut, fashionably short. She'd decided on a dress with a low neckline. Her breasts were her best feature. Everyone said so, the men happily, the women bitchily. Okay, maybe she was a bit overweight, but it was only the women who sneered, and she could live with that.

Her worst feature, she knew, was her tongue. It was too sharp for its own good, but it was defended by a dimpled smile that she had perfected in her teens so that few took offense. Those who did weren't worth bothering with;

that had been her rule of thumb all her adult life and it had stood her in good stead.

She was deliberately late; she hated being one of the first at these functions. The later you were, the more chance you had of finding someone you could talk to.

"Darling," she was welcomed by someone she couldn't place. She picked up a drink and began to mingle, her smile nicely in place, pecking at cheeks, looking around for anyone she knew. Normally the point of the exercise at these functions was to get work, but now that she had the muscle of Jack Mason behind her, she was secure for a while, and happily smug.

"Miss Brompton?"

The voice at her elbow was deep and heavily accented. Italian, she thought as she swung round and looked up into a young, brown face. Handsome but not too handsome. Young but probably too damned young. She was polite with her good evening as he introduced himself as Francis.

"Francis who?"

He shrugged, pretending not to notice the question. He was, she noticed, the only one in the room without a glass in his hand.

"You *are* Miss Brompton?"

She nodded, intrigued. There was something un-publishing about him, unfashionable and somehow—she searched for the word—unworldly. And why was she singled out? There were far younger and prettier women in the room.

"And you are working on a book about the Thorns."

Anna blinked and spluttered into her glass. How on earth did he know?

"I read about you in the paper. The *Standard*."

"Ah."

The daily had gotten wind of the story and had run a couple of paragraphs that day.

"And I called your number. The machine said you were here."

Now she was curious, asked who he was, where he was from.

"There is a word for it," he said seriously. "About crashing fences or something."

She smiled at him. It was no trouble gate-crashing a publishing party, if you felt like it. But why? In answer he patted his jacket and asked her to move to a quieter spot with him for a moment.

"It is as you say a life-or-death matter."

Her imagination did a double-take—an Italian patting his jacket and leading her astray. Hit men in the movies were usually handsome, but he was only pulling an envelope from his pocket as they reached a spot by the window away from the throng.

"I do not expect you to believe my story," he said. "I have tried to tell it before without success."

Anna opened her mouth to speak but he held

up a hand for silence, and she blinked at him again. Curiouser and curiouser.

"All you need to know is that I have been involved with the Thorn people all my life. As an outsider, you understand. In the past I have tried to warn people and all I have met is disbelief. Eventually people believe, but by then they are doomed."

Anna laughed. It was such an absurd word. Doomed, indeed. But there was no stopping him now, not even if she had wanted to.

"If I tell you what I know, you won't believe me. You will say I am . . ." He paused, thinking of the phrase, then smiled for the first time. "You will say I am insulting your intelligence."

"I can take it," Anna said, trying for flippancy, but he frowned at her remark.

"All I ask is you read this," he said earnestly, patting the envelope. "Inside is a list of people who have been involved with the Thorns. I have marked those that I knew myself or met briefly. There is a common link."

Anna grabbed it greedily, slit it open with her thumbnail, and pulled out the contents. Some of the names were familiar, others she had never heard of. It was a long list. Each name had a sentence of description. She had hardly started reading when he told her the link. "Every one of these people has died violently or disappeared."

Anna did not look up. "But this is marvelous."

Francis blinked. It was hardly the reaction he had expected.

Her eyes flicked to the top of the list, and then she turned the page and looked at the last name. From someone called Chessa to Paul Buher. When she looked up, her eyes were bright with excitement.

"May I keep this?"

"Of course. That is the whole point."

She stood on tiptoe and kissed him on the cheek, saw him flinch. "I don't know who you are, Signor Francis, my lamb, or where you've come from, but I am very grateful. Now, what I suggest is that we go have some supper and you can tell me more about these people." She searched in her handbag, wondering whether she had brought her notebook, then felt his hand on her arm, the fingers gripping tightly, and it was her turn to flinch. She looked up to protest and saw him glaring at her and shaking his head.

"Listen. These people are victims of the Thorn disease. This list is a warning so that you do not catch it. I'm telling you. It's impossible to crash the Thorn fences."

She tried to smile, her seductive, charming let's-not-be-silly smile, but it was no good. Francis was shaking her, making her spill her wine. People were looking across at them.

"I beg you," he said. "I am not being melodramatic. If you interfere, you will join the list. If you think I'm crazy, just check it out and calculate the mathematical odds. Why should each one die violently? Then ask yourself: 'Why should I be different?' ''

Then he was gone, pushing his way through the crowd, oblivious to their mumbled protests. For a moment she watched him go, then looked down at the piece of paper.

"Jesus," she said softly. "What luck."

She left the party as soon as was politely possible, refusing offers of dinner by various groups. Those who had seen her with the Italian made the standard leering comments. There would be bitchery and rumor-mongering going on behind her. She knew that and did not care. Indeed, it was quite flattering to be thought of as going off on an assignation with this tall dark stranger. Had they known that she was going to the BBC's microfilm library in Shepherds Bush, they would not have believed her, and she did not mind that either.

Anna worked through the night, oblivious to the passage of time, checking names on the list against the news stories. Chessa, a young nanny to the three-year-old Damien Thorn, had thrown herself out of a top-story window with a rope around her neck. Verdict suicide, motive unknown.

Then the Thorns themselves; Kathy and Robert,

then a photographer, a priest, a group of Italian monks, friends, relatives, strangers, all mysteries.

From Chicago to London, death and destruction, and never an explanation. As the man had said, it was a disease. More than that, a plague, some kind of virus.

It was early morning when she left, red-eyed, carrying a sheaf of notes, exhilarated despite her exhaustion. In the cab on the way home, she checked her watch. It was the middle of the night in New York, but she couldn't wait to pass on the information. She would telex it from home even if it meant staying up until noon.

It was not until she got to her room that she remembered Francis' words—"Why should I be different?"—and the first tremors of apprehension hit her, followed by a panic that maybe she'd never find him again.

She looked at the envelope and sighed with relief. He had written his name and phone number on the back. It was more than just neat, it was a minor work of art, a sort of old-fashioned copperplate. It looked as though it had been written with a quill pen, and she wondered what sort of man in the year 2001 would bother to make his phone number look pretty?

‹§ CHAPTER 6 §›

JACK MASON READ the telex over breakfast with a growing sense of amazement tinged with admiration for his researcher. At the end, after the paragraph on the suicide of Paul Buher, he ripped the sheet from the machine.

"Signing off now," he read, "and going to sleep. Please leave acknowledgement/congratulations for eight hours. Anna."

Mason caressed the paper, drawing his fingers down it as if it were silk. It was certainly worth more than silk. In all his fantasies about the Thorns, he could never have imagined such a catalogue of tragedy. He counted thirty-two names and shook his head in astonishment. Whoever or whatever had affected the Thorns was more malignant than any disease.

Such a list, if checked out, provided the chapter plan for the book. All he needed to do now was add the flesh. He picked up the phone to dial London, then changed his mind. She had asked not to be disturbed, and her request should be respected. Instead he phoned TWA and booked himself on the next flight to Chicago, then called his friend on the *Times* to get the cuttings on the Chicago men on Anna's list.

Less than two hours later he was heading northwest at twenty thousand feet, immersed once more in the message from London. Who the hell was Haber Jennings? Or Father Thomas Doolan? Or a priest called Tassone? What had they done to incur the wrath of whatever afflicted those connected with the Thorns? Jennings beheaded by a pane of glass, Doolan buried alive, Tassone crucified?

Mason was a betting man, and he had picked up on a line from Anna about the strange young Italian. Calculate the odds, he had said: an impossible task for your local bookmaker but an interesting task for a computer. He made a mental note to feed in the information. Meanwhile he had a town to see.

Jack Mason was a writer who needed to visit the places he was describing, to get the feel of the atmosphere. He wanted to absorb the Thorns by osmosis, to wander their streets and sniff out their houses. He did not believe in ghosts, but he believed in the power of that phenomenon called inspiration.

One day soon he would have to sit at his typewriter and pray that the words would come—inspired words, forced through the brain into the fingers, words that would make the book something that would move people and not simply a dry exercise of the intellect. The Thorns had to come alive again, and whatever virus that infected them had to be the villain of the piece.

Two hours later, after staring at the derelict site that had once housed the Thorn Museum, burned down in 1963 and left as rubble, he walked through the gates of the cemetery on the North Side and gazed at the Thorn Mausoleum. It was a circular granite building with massive oak doors, a memorial to four generations of Thorns, when the mortal remains of Damien, the most illustrious, lay, dead at his prime.

He shivered as he reached the place, touched the polished granite, felt it burn his palm, pulled it away quickly so that the skin would not stick to the frozen stone, then pushed the door. It did not move. It may have once been open for public inspection, but no longer. The bones and the memories of the Thorn family were sealed inside, closed off to the curiosity of strangers.

Mason grunted in annoyance. He had wanted to see the place, to fix it in his mind, and he wondered whom he would need to see to apply for permission.

He turned, feeling the cold fog from the lake penetrate his coat and seep into the marrow of his bones. He ignored it and slowly wandered back through the cemetery, stopping to scan the stones.

There was a double headstone for a couple named Cartwright. He glanced at it and moved on, thinking of his two ex-wives, wondering grimly what it would be like to be interred with both of them for eternity, a strange ménage-á-trois to be sure, then remembered something from Anna's list. It was here that the priest named Doolan had died a gruesome death. He had fallen into an open grave one night over a year ago and broken his back, then someone had buried him alive.

Another mystery. No one had been charged. No one was ever charged in the Thorn saga. Since then the conspiracy theorists had had their inevitable say. They pointed to scratch marks by the grave, but their conclusions were laughed out of sight.

Mason wandered across to the grave which now contained its rightful occupant, the woman for whom it had been dug. Doolan had been disinterred and reburied. As he looked down, he shuddered and felt cold again.

"Psychosomatic," he said to himself and turned away, glancing again at the cutting. A barman was quoted, saying that the priest had been drinking that evening. Mason squinted up the path to the street, saw the sign:

O'Lunney's Bar and Grill

Suddenly he was thirsty.

He was on his second scotch when he decided to produce the cutting. The barman, fat and bald, squinted at it and nodded.

"You're Mason, aintchya?"

Mason groaned, silently cursing his ego that had made him do all those TV programs.

"Read two of yer books. Not bad."

"Thanks. Now can you tell me about the priest?"

Again the barman shrugged. "Been at the holy water," he said. "Rambling an' raving. Had a metal detector with him, kept going on about somebody's bones not being in their grave. One of the Thorns."

The barman laughed, and it was an ugly sight.

"Did you tell the police this?"

"Huh, and wind up wearing an overcoat back to front?" He laughed again.

An hour later Mason left, his thirst unchecked, his curiosity doing cartwheels. There were only questions in this story and no answers. Not yet, anyway.

The next name on the list lived in one of the

suburbs. Janet Finn was a small, gray-haired woman with a face that seemed set in grief.

She let him in without a second thought and listened to what he had to say, then nodded and showed him around the house. One room was a study, every wall covered in books—old tomes, biblical and historical.

"This is where Michael worked," she said softly. "He was just an academic, you know. He rarely moved from here. I brought him coffee every hour on the hour."

Slowly she explained that some eighteen or so years earlier he had discovered a set of daggers in an auction. He had been terribly excited about them and persuaded a priest named Doolan to take them to Italy.

"I don't know why," she said. "I never asked. It wasn't that I wasn't interested, it was just that he kept to himself, and his work. Then it was forgotten, until last year, when he read about the daggers in a magazine and decided to go to England."

She smiled. "He'd never been abroad before. I told him to be careful."

The smile failed her, and Mason knew that the tears were not far behind.

"I shouldn't have let him go, but what can you do? Then he phoned and said he'd found something out that was very important and that he'd seen the ambassador . . ."

"Philip Brennan?" Mason asked quickly.

She nodded. "It was all too much for him, moving in such circles. Books, that's all Michael knew, and there he was jetting around like that."

She paused to wipe away a tear, then smiled up at him, bravely trying to tell the story as if the memories were not tearing her apart.

"I went to the airport to meet him, all the way to New York. I thought it would be nice. That's the worst part, remembering the plane coming in. Of course, at the time I didn't know . . ."

Her bravery faltered, and she sagged against him. Mason knew the story well, how the poor man had somehow fallen onto one of the wheels as the plane came in to land. It had been a mystery how he got into the wheel bay in the first place. Yet another mystery, and briefly Mason wondered what they had found of him to bury.

It was time to leave; time to call Anna in London. He thanked the woman and walked smartly down the road, turned the corner, and saw her standing in the doorway waving, just as she must have waved that day at Kennedy Airport.

❧ CHAPTER 7 ❧

IT WAS THE loneliness that was the worst thing, even harder to bear than the fear. Francis could just about cope with the fear, at least during the day when he concentrated on practical matters. He knew that if he stopped to think about the forces he was up against, he would weaken and run for the sanctuary of home.

He felt so small and insignificant. At least Father De Carlo, when he had made this journey almost twenty years ago, had had six men with him. As he thought about the priest, he trembled. The old man, at the end, had described those days repeatedly, how they had been brought the seven sacred daggers of Meggido, the only weapons that could destroy the Antichrist, how the others had perished and how, finally, the last dagger had been driven into the body of Damien Thorn.

The old man had thought that the sacrifice of the others had not been in vain, that the mission had been accomplished, only to learn later that although the body of Thorn had been destroyed, his spirit lived through the son.

They had been ignorant of the lessons of the prophet, that to destroy the satanic spirit, all seven daggers had to be planted in the body, and in a particular pattern, in the shape of the cross.

The knowledge of his failure had almost driven the old man mad, but he at least had not died alone. At the end, he still had the faithful Brother Francis.

It was a blasphemous thought. Francis kept telling himself he could never be alone, not when he had his God, not when the figure of Christ walked the land, but even as he prayed, he knew that this was not enough. What he needed was someone with whom he could share the burden.

That morning he had prayed on his knees for an hour until the cramps in his calves stopped him, then he had washed himself carefully and put on clean clothes, feeling suddenly like some sort of virginal sacrifice. He had giggled to himself at the thought, but the laughter was not born out of amusement. It came from terror.

Before leaving, he listened again to the tape-recorded voice of Paul Buher. By now he knew every inflection, every pause for breath. He knew what had to be done, because Buher had spelled it out, telling where the daggers were and what had to be done with them. He had not needed to listen again to the old man's voice, but it was company, the voice of someone who knew—even if it came from beyond the grave.

The tape came to an end, and he snapped on the radio to check the time. A newscaster was talking about a buildup of forces on the Russian-Chinese border, of notes of protest being exchanged, of heightened tension, the failure of an initiative from the White House, of the United Nations going into emergency session once more; on and on, the same old chorus. Only the date had changed.

Francis sighed and touched the crucifix around his neck. It was time to go. He left the small room and was on his way out when the landlady called from the hall. There was a phone call for him. From a woman.

He thanked her and picked up the receiver, looked at it, feeling uncomfortable. He wasn't accustomed to telephones. There were none at Subiaco. They were not considered necessary.

It was Anna. Immediately he felt himself blush, a strange thought flashing through his mind that those moist lips by the telephone could be only an inch from his face. She was asking to see him, giving him her address, saying it was important, maybe they could have dinner.

When he hung up, he was trembling. No one had ever spoken to him in that way before. The word was "seductive." No one had ever talked seductively to him, because everyone knew who he was and respected his vows. But she only knew him as Francis. There would be temptation of the flesh at the address he had scribbled on the phone book, and he prayed that he had the strength to resist.

It was midday by the time he reached the Pereford lodge, and he was shivering with cold and tension. He could see someone in uniform by the lodge gate looking at him as he walked past. He returned the man's gaze and walked on, thinking of Buher's words, some of which he had had to look up in the dictionary. The idea of electronic detection units and a need for surveillance amazed him, and again the enormity of the task frightened him.

He knew nothing of reconnoitering, or any such thing. His skills were in Latin and carpentry. It was fine for Buher to say that the daggers were in the church inside the grounds and to warn about electronic surveillance, but from what he had said, it would need a small army to get in and do the job.

Instinctively Francis looked at the sky and prayed for inspiration. If there was no divine guidance, then he had no chance. As he moved off slowly along the east wall, his breath froze around him, a litany of Latin mumbled aloud.

The security guard's hand hovered over the phone.

Bill Jeffries was an observant man, but he had not noticed the tension in the room. He was briefing Damien on a meeting of foreign ministers in Peking when he looked up. The dog had come into the drawing room unnoticed and was staring at Damien, hackles raised, whimpering. Damien was holding the stare, feeling the scars on his neck, and Jeffries felt queasy. Was it his imagination or was there something unhealthy about this silent communion?

"Damien?" He touched the young man's arm, then stepped back as Damien turned. His eyes were slits, his breath was foul, and Jeffries could barely make out the word, a strange biblical term, repeated in a whisper:

"Nazarene."

Jeffries did not know what to say or do. The question, when it came, sounded so inept— "What's the matter, Damien?" As if he had just sneezed or something.

Then the boy was striding from the room, the dog behind him, and Jeffries moved nearer the fire, feeling a sudden chill. He glanced at the leather-bound report from which he had been reading. A moment ago it had seemed the most important thing in the world, but now it seemed irrelevant. Damien's expression had frightened him. The hell with Peking, he thought, and reached for the brandy.

It was George who found him praying in the black chapel. Instinctively the old man knew when he was needed, and now was the time. The dog stood back to let him pass, and the old man stood in the doorway, saw the tears run down Damien's face, and felt a tremor of pity. Only he knew of the young man's terrible loneliness. Damien had not asked for this task, and it was to his credit that he had turned his loneliness into a wonderful obsession. He was going to destroy the world, to free mankind from the eternal choice between good and evil. The destruction would come as a relief. Man was to be put out of his misery. It would be the peace of the dead.

Damien turned slowly and looked up at him, then got to his feet.

"I feel His blessed power, old man," he said. "The Nazarene stalks me again."

"As it was written."

Damien nodded, then walked past him, motioning him to follow. It was a strange procession, the young man in his cassock, the old man bent and wheezing, the dog panting at the rear. They crossed the lawn and made their way slowly up the hill to the church.

A few yards from the gate, Damien stopped and clasped the old man's hand.

"It was here that you found the sign," he said.

"Not me, sir. I knew nothing of the growth in the belly of the beast."

"Nonetheless, you did well." His tone changed to one of compassion. "You have not much longer on this earth."

George nodded.

"You will be well rewarded."

George turned his head away so that Damien would not see his fear. Ever since he had reached these last days, he had been besieged with feelings of doubt. He knew what it was—that benign influence that had reached out to so many, including Buher, that obscene craving for repentance. Worse, he knew that Damien knew, for there were no secrets; so why was he torturing him with this promise of damnation, unless it was a bad joke?

When he looked up, Damien had turned and was standing at the gate, staring at the church, and the old man was reminded of the night of Armageddon when Buher had destroyed the spirit of them all and young Damien had been unable to do anything to stop him. Like his father, he had never had the courage to step onto hallowed ground, and the old man knew the torture he felt, that terrible combination of fear and guilt.

And then he was taking it out in roars of anger at the ruined building and the desecrated crucifix inside.

"Nazarene, you still think you can defeat me!" His words echoed around the ruin and bellowed back at him. "Your thousand years of peace are a mockery. Mankind is more malignant than ever. The cancer in his brain is about to destroy him. The warmongers have inherited the earth, Nazarene. . . ."

As he listened, George felt the now familiar nausea and the dizziness and the pain across his chest. He stared at Damien's back, concentrating on the one spot, knowing that he could not faint, not now when Damien was railing against his adversary.

George could not do anything that might interrupt in case he intruded, in case his dying would irritate the young man, and so he stood trembling as Damien roared obscenities into the church until he had exhausted himself.

He was quieter now. "Another feeble emissary," he said. "Where do you find them, Nazarene? Another monk to follow all these men and women of honor. You send him after me as you sent others after my father, in the sure knowledge that they are doomed. What manner of hypocrisy is this? What pleasure do you take from their destruction? Is it their miserable souls that you want, their immortal souls, cleansed by their blood and their petty sacrifices, so that they can sit at your right hand and be pampered?'

He turned and stared across the fields. "It is so meaningless," he said softly. "He is already destroyed, and this one is not even dangerous, only misguided."

Half a mile away, Francis stood by the gate of the east wall, peering through the bars, and shivered, thinking he could see something, two pinpricks of yellow in the distance, and his prayers stuck in his throat.

❧ CHAPTER 8 ❧

FOR THREE NIGHTS Francis had little sleep. It was as it had been when he was young, when he had been tempted by the holy pictures in his mother's Bible, when he read the word "harlot" again and again and the stories of the wicked women bruising their breasts against men, when he had even lusted after paintings of the Madonna—all things that he had never been able to confess, not even years later to Father De Carlo.

And now the temptation was back in the shape of Anna. Her face, her exposed breasts, tortured him each night in dreams, half awake, half asleep, then he woke exhausted each morning, clutching himself and coated with guilt.

The days, if anything, were worse. He took the train each morning to the country and walked to the big house, stared through the bars, trying to force his mind to think, then, defeated, he returned to London.

He had found a small church in a back street, and he prayed for guidance, thinking of the old stories, of David slaying Goliath, of Christ rising from the dead to claim a kingdom of the minds of men and women, of the promise that the forces of darkness would be cast down, no matter how long it took, which was all very well, but he still had no idea how he was going to get past the cameras and into the church before he was caught by the dogs. And when he looked up at the cross by the altar, it seemed to him that the image of Christ stared back at him in pity.

There was no guidance. He was on his own.

On the fourth night, it happened again. He awoke from a nightmare, of Anna's lips around him, sucking and biting. He shivered and swung out of bed, pulled on his robe, and ran to the bathroom along the corridor. He slipped off the robe and stood under the shower, washing away his guilt, closing his eyes against the spray and whatever he might see in the mirror, for he remembered the priest's warning, that Satan had the power over men's minds, that the Beast sought out the weakest points, the simplest route to temptation, and so often, such a route was the most predictable.

Eyes shut, he groped his way back to bed, slipped between the sheets, and stretched out. It was the smell he was first aware of, a heavy, sweet smell not unlike incense, then the touch of flesh against him and the sound of her voice in his ear, murmuring terrible things, obscenities.

He pressed his lips together and screwed his eyes tight, tried to reach for his crucifix around his neck, but something was in the way, something soft and damp. He roared, pushed his way out of the suffocating sheets, ran from the room, and cowered in the corridor, his knees pulled up to his chest, arms clasped round them, his face turned against the wall, and it was in this position that his landlady found him next morning.

She nodded as he stammered a reply that he had been sleepwalking, but she wasn't convinced, not at the sight of so many deep bruises on his neck, the kind that the common people called lovebites.

Anna was annoyed at being stood up by the Italian. She had tidied up the flat and bought some Frascati and Valpolicella to give him a choice and make him feel at home: but nothing, not even a phone call to apologize. Then, when he did show up, in the middle of the afternoon, she wasn't ready for him. No makeup, hair a mess, fresh from the shower, half in and half out of her bathrobe, but she managed a welcoming smile and stood back to let him in.

He looked different, as if he hadn't slept for a week, the suntan faded to khaki. Still, he had arrived. Jack would be pleased she'd found him again.

She tried for small talk, hoped he liked the flat. They called it the jungle, she said, because of all the plants. She offered drinks, said she was sorry to be such a mess but—

"Listen, I'm going away tomorrow," he said.

"Ah."

'And I want to repeat something I told a brave man the last time I was in London, that he would consider me crazy if I told him what I knew.'

Anna grunted impatiently. This was a replay of the other night. She wished he would get to the point and stop staring like a schoolboy at her cleavage. She crossed her arms and waited.

"If I say I am going on a mission and that I am the only one who can do this thing, then please believe me."

"Yes, but—"

"If I say I may die, you will think I'm being melodramatic."

"Oh for Chrissake, Francis." She was getting sick of all this, and without thinking, she placed her hands on her hips in a pose of annoyance. Her robe fell open. Francis blinked, closed his eyes, turned away for a moment. When he turned back, he was holding a package.

"I ask you to keep this," he said, looking into her face and offering it. She took it, a mailing bag sealed with red wax.

"If I don't return, open this." he said. "Then you will forget all about this Thorn business. I'm sure of it."

She shook her head and was about to tell him he was being ridiculous when he placed his hands on her shoulders.

"Just remember," he said. "Everyone who has taken the route I am taking is dead. If I join the list, promise me you will hand these over to the authorites."

"Well, that depends."

"Promise me," he said, squeezing her, hurting her. "Promise that you will forget the Thorns." His intensity frightened her, and her fear instantly turned to anger. She struggled with him and tried to pull away.

"Promise!" It was a roar, a frenzied demand.

"Fuck off," she said.

The word hit him like a punch in the teeth. He stepped back and shook his head, raising one hand toward her, as if to caress her.

"Oh no," she said, angry now. "You've got no sense of timing, my friend." Then he leaped at her, grabbing at her body, his mouth at her neck, but she was ready for him, bringing her knee up fast, hearing him gasp, then she stepped back and looked down at him.

"Get out."

He got to his feet and backed away, shaking his head, the tears forming. Whether it was pain or humiliation she did not know, nor did she care.

"Anna, I'm sorry," he said. "Oh, mother of God, forgive me."

"Get out," she said again. "You're pathetic."

And he was gone, backing out of the door in tears as she reached for the phone to call the police.

Now there was no longer any uncertainty. Francis knew exactly what had to be done. He would simply climb the wall and rush for the church, take his chance with the dogs and get the daggers, in the blind faith that God would be with him; if not, then it would be over.

He no longer cared what happened to him, not after what he had done. He had acted worse than the beasts, and there could be no forgiveness. As he walked through the streets, he mumbled a prayer in Latin and hoped that God was not turning a deaf ear to him.

He had no idea how he got to the terrible place known as Soho. One moment he was on his way to his room, the next he was in the middle of a godforsaken neighborhood with neon signs advertising all manner of sins. Men were calling to him to follow them down dirty corridors. Painted women were trying to entice him to come with them.

He must have taken a wrong turn. He could

not believe such places existed and vaguely wondered why the authorities allowed it.

A fat woman leered at him and asked if he wanted some company. Francis backed off, making the sign of the cross. The whores were not even pretty. That was the confusion. Most of them were repulsive, but even their repulsiveness attracted him. It was a contradiction, and he could not understand it. He had no knowledge of the world, no ammunition except his vows and his faith.

And so he prayed as he stumbled along the crowded pavements, mumbling Latin, hands clasped together. Most people ignored him; those who registered his presence simply assumed that he was another victim.

He seemed to be walking in circles, kept seeing the same street signs—Brewer, Frith, Greek, Berwick—and narrow alleys, seemingly skyless. He was jostled and pushed. Bodies were pressed against him. He heard curses and entreaties, offers and propositions.

Stumbling out of an alley into a small square, he thought he saw the shape of a massive dog staring at him malevolently, and then the crowd swayed around him again, carrying him forward. When he stopped, pushed against a hoarding, he looked up to see a gaudy poster advertising a movie, a woman with Anna's face and exposed breasts smiling at him. He smelled the perfume again and felt the sweet sting of her teeth on his neck and he ran blindly, heedless of the curses of the barrow boys and the screeches of the whores.

It was dark by the time he reached the house. The place was silent and empty, and he was glad. He did not want to see anyone. All he wanted was to collect his belongings and get out to the country where the air was fresh and empty of temptation.

He was panting as he reached his room and pulled the door open. He half fell inside, closed his eyes, and slammed it behind him. Slowly he drew deep breaths, trying to calm himself, then he stiffened. He was not alone. Someone was breathing in harmony with him, the deep grunting of a man and the higher pitch of a woman.

Murmuring a prayer, he reached for his crucifix, but when he touched it, he felt the texture of skin, as if the cross were flesh, reaching erect for his throat. He shivered and forced himself to open his eyes.

Anna lay on his bed, face down, a young man on top of her. Both were naked, the young man thrusting at her. Francis groaned and slumped against the door and they both turned to stare at him. Frances recognized the face. The boy was the double of pictures he had seen of the young Damien Thorn, and he was grinning at him. In his imagination, Francis thought the eyes were yellow, animal eyes without irises.

Anna had twisted onto her side and was urging him to come to them, to join in, to take her, saying words he did not understand.

He shook his head violently and forced himself to look away, to the far wall, where he had hung the big two-foot-long crucifix he had taken from Subiaco. It was gone. Then he saw it, lying in the corner, smashed, as if someone had flung it at the wall. One of the crossbeams had snapped off, and the base had broken into a jagged splinter.

Francis leaped for it, grabbed it by the head of Christ, and turned back toward the bed. The boy was sneering at him, dripping saliva, and Francis was aware of the smell of him—musk, an animal smell, the odor of a zoo. Instinctively he knew now what he had to do. The daggers could wait.

"Father give me strength," he whispered as he raised the crucifix. He saw the boy's grin widen, saw the sharp canines as he brought it down with all his strength. Anna screamed, and he caught a glimpse of her nakedness, then the crucifix smashed into the sneering mouth, splintering the teeth, gouging through the gums and tongue, deep down into the throat. It lodged in the gullet, and Francis felt the boy's pain, tasted his blood, felt the choking begin as the crucifix cut off air.

Yet still the yellow eyes stared at him as if in triumph. The bile rose in Francis' throat, and the obscenity of what he had done made him retch and fight for breath. As he dropped to his knees, he thought he saw Anna smile, then her hand was reaching for him, her nails painted black, the obscenities still vomiting from her lips.

It was the landlady who found him, and she went immediately into shock. The sergeant who responded to the call was the type who boasted that he had seen it all and that nothing could shake him, but it was too much even for him. He vomited at the sight and again in the station when he was describing it to the desk sergeant. It was two hours before he could compose himself to write out his report, and as he typed it, he tried to imagine what kind of sick mind could think up such a way of dealing death.

❧ CHAPTER 9 ❧

ANNA HAD SPENT the day at the BBC library and was so preoccupied with her work that she paid no attention to the two women on the Tube train gossiping over the latest sick murder. London was far worse than New York now, they were saying. Whoever heard of such a thing, killing someone with a crucifix?

Vaguely she registered them reveling in their disgust, blaming the murder on everything from the weather to the Chinese and the violence on television. But she took no notice of them. She was too busy concentrating on the idea of a jinx, some malign force that attached itself to certain people or groups of people and never left them.

She knew all about being accident-prone. Anna had realized since she was a kid that she was the type that attracted minor disasters. Screwdrivers slipped. Hammerheads flew off. Any horse she backed would lead up until the last fence. If she fell in love, he would go off with her best friend. She was an accident waiting to happen. Maybe the Thorns were just an extension of this phenomenon, carried to the ultimate.

She was musing on this possibility in the flat, half listening to the news, when she heard the words: "Police are regarding this as one of the most brutal murders they have encountered."

She glanced idly at the screen, then sat up startled, as she gazed into the face of Francis, and still did not fully comprehend, even as the report continued: "Scotland Yard has issued this passport photo of the monk and are appealing to anyone who might have met him. . . ."

The phone rang. It was a friend who had been at the publishing party, asking if it was the young Italian she had been talking to. Still she did not take it all in. It was only when she had put the phone down that she understood, and even then her mind dealt with irrelevancies. A monk. Now his behavior made some kind of sense.

The TV was on automatic video, and she spun the tape back and froze it on the unsmiling face of the dead man, stared at the brown eyes, thinking of his warning, telling her to stay clear of the Thorns. As she gazed at him, she felt fear for the first time. The list had lengthened by another name, and the odds against coincidence had shortened still further.

Then the tears came, mixed emotions of sadness and fear, and a terrible regret that although she had met him only twice, she had rejected him so brutally. Her last words, "You're pathetic," echoed in her mind as she looked at him. Pathetic indeed, and it was a full half hour before she could compose herself sufficiently to call the police.

The interview lasted an hour. She had not told them about the death list, only that he had warned her off the Thorn book. They took their notes, concealing their confusion with a display of efficiency. It helped that she had worked with policemen before and knew how to treat them. She also knew they were baffled.

Back in her flat she realized that she hadn't told them about the package. She wasn't being evasive, it was simply that in her state of shock, she had forgotten about it. Now it was another morbid reminder, lying on her desk, the red wax seal seeming to wink at her.

Her fingers trembled as she fought with it, thinking of the last thing the policeman had said, that the murderer must be psychotic because no sane man would ram a crucifix down someone's throat. There was no motive, no forced entry to the flat. The only forced entry had been to Francis' throat.

It was an obscene joke, but they had both laughed. Humor knew no morality, and the ugly play on words helped to clear the tension a little.

She winced as she cut her finger on the tape, then tore savagely at the packet, her blood smearing the wax. It opened suddenly and four tape cassettes fell onto the desk, then she pulled out a sheaf of letters. A note from Francis was stapled to them:

"Just assume these are the ravings of lunatics. That way, it will be easier for you. These are copies I have made from the original letters."

It was the same copperplate handwriting, beautifully crafted, and she sat down to read. The first was from a woman called Kate Reynolds to Father De Carlo. She knew the name well. It was halfway down the list. It was a crazy letter, as Francis said, the ravings of a madwoman, but an astonishingly lucid madwoman. Then there was another, from a woman called Lamont, another name from the list.

Anna read slowly, trying not to analyze what she was reading. It was, as Francis said, crazy. So crazy that Mason could not possibly do his book. He would be an object of derision and his career would be ruined. Finally, there was a long series of notes and biblical references written by the priest in a wavering hand, all about the Second Coming of Christ and the Jews returning to Zion, how Christ would meet his Antichrist at the Battle of Armageddon.

She read this with increasing irritation; she knew enough of all this from the fundamentalists. The U.S. government had been riddled with such people for years, from James Watt, the Secretary of the Interior in the 1980s, through to the present incumbent. They called themselves millennialists. Anna swore. If Mason were to link the Thorns with the Book of Revelation, then he'd never find another publisher. They'd think the strain had finally gotten to him.

At last she slipped the first cassette into her tape deck and sat back to listen.

"Father, forgive the way I speak." An old, distorted voice. Anna closed her eyes and slumped in her chair, but when she heard the name Paul Buher, she sat up fast, her irritation immediately evaporating and replaced by new enthusiasm. If this was really Buher, then she had something to show Mason.

A moment later she was searching her desk for Francis' list as the old voice crackled through the room.

"In memoriam. Chessa Whyte . . ."

It was the same. She leaned forward, on the edge of her seat, biting her fingernails, staring at the machine as if this would make her hear better. Then, as the confession continued, she slowly sat back in her chair, closed her eyes, and sighed.

More sacred daggers. More Armageddons, more Antichrists. More madness.

She listened for two hours, then packed the cassettes and the letters in the file marked "Thorn" and picked up the phone.

Mason was out. She left a message and wandered around the room, trying to think what to do next. The answer was simple. Carry on until told otherwise. She was still on the payroll, so she would go through the motions.

She wound the first tape back to the list of names. Buher had added another. Margaret Brennan, the only one still alive. There was an address, a hospital in Highgate.

Again Anna reached for the phone, thinking that with a bit of luck, they wouldn't allow her to visit.

The hospital was a half-hour cab ride from Anna's flat, but the journey felt like half a day. As she got nearer, she wished she had left this particular chore to Jack Mason. She dreaded hospitals. Her mother had died in a hospice for the mentally ill, and Anna had never fully recovered from the trauma. She had been there at the end, and it had been a terrible death, her mother screaming despite the drugs, her last expression one of terror as if she had glimpsed the hereafter and was horrified by it.

Now she wished she had taken some Dutch courage in the hope that the nurses wouldn't smell it, or Valium maybe, but it was against her professional nature. She needed to be alert during interviews; she couldn't sit grinning at the poor woman like the Cheshire Cat.

At least the area was pretty. It would have been worse somehow if the place had been built in some depressing slum area—not that it would have made much difference to the patients, but somehow it made it more acceptable to her.

When the cab driver pulled up and nodded toward the building, Anna shivered. It hadn't occurred to her that St. Ignatius would be a convent.

She let herself out and stood looking at a twelve-foot-high wall and a heavy oak double door with spikes on the top. The electric bell and the spyhole somehow seemed out of place.

Knock three times and ask for the saint, she thought irreverently as she hit the bell and heard chimes in the distance.

A small trapdoor slid open, showing a pair of brown eyes beneath a black hood.

Anna gave her name and said she'd called for an appointment. The grille closed, then the door creaked open and Anna stepped inside. The courtyard was a square of concrete with no concession to comfort: no chairs, no plants, nothing alive, only a procession of nuns in black habits walking the perimeter. Anna was reminded of a prison yard.

Silence and the smell of morphine.

The nun gestured silently for her to follow, and she crossed the courtyard toward the hospital, a dark place with the outlines of the patients at each small window, a series of profiles, motionless as if they had been painted.

Anna looked back and up at the sky, blue and fresh. The outside world seemed a hundred miles away, and now she could hear chanting as they approached the main door, a dull monotone, low-pitched for women and, to Anna's mind, heavy with despair.

As she reached the door she scolded herself for her presumption. Who was she to accuse them of despair, these brides of Christ? They had made their peace with this world and the next. It was not for her to judge.

The building was cool, with flagstone floors and green-tiled walls that made the faces of the nuns looked sickly. No one spoke or looked at her as she moved behind her guide along the main corridor, then down another and finally down a set of steps.

Anna touched the wall and immediately drew back, thinking she felt damp. She looked at her fingers, but it was just her imagination running away with her.

The nun stopped by a door, unlocked it, and pushed it open. For a moment Anna did not move. There had been no questions asked. No one wanted to know why she wanted to see Margaret Brennan. She had assumed it would be difficult. She wasn't a relative or even a friend, yet there was no interrogation. It was as if they did not care.

She stepped inside and twitched, startled, as the door clanged behind her. The room was no more than a narrow cell, just a cot, a chair, and a table. The window was set high at ground level, and Margaret Brennan sat beneath it, her back to the door, staring at the wall. She was wearing a white tunic and seemed oblivious to Anna's presence.

Anna coughed, but still the woman did not turn. Slowly she crossed the room, stopped two feet from her, and gently spoke her name.

The woman turned, and Anna stifled a cry. The face was prematurely old, haggard, lined, white-haired, the eyes bulbous and staring. The photos in the press had not prepared Anna for anything like this. The woman of a year ago had been radiant, shiny-haired, with a wicked smile. This was an old woman. The word "crone" leaped to Anna's mind, and she mentally swallowed it, fixed a smile that she hoped wasn't a grimace and tried again.

"Mrs. Brennan, my name is Anna Brompton."

She smiled, and her face creased like paper.

"How nice of you to come."

It was a cultured Boston accent and reminded Anna of the Kennedys. She took the hand that was offered and again had to swallow her revulsion. The skin was dry and crackled at the touch.

"It's nice this time of year," said Margaret. "The flowers smell beautiful."

Anna nodded, wondering how she was going to get her onto the subject of the Thorns, wondering just why she was here, whether it was legitimate research or morbid curiosity.

Normally she just let people speak, say what came into their heads, before steering them to the point at issue. But this wasn't normal.

"You must be wondering why I came."

Margaret smiled. "No. I understand." She turned away and gazed once more at the wall.

"I'm working for a man called Jack Mason."

No response.

"You may have heard of him—"

"The writer?" Margaret turned back. "Of course. I believe I met him once, at a party in New York."

This was a piece of luck. Anna smiled. "Yes, well, you see, he is planning a book on the Thorn family . . ."

The mood changed. Margaret frowned and shook her head as if she had been hit, then turned away.

"It's a sort of dynastic book," Anna continued. "You see, he's fascinated by them, by their—"

"Damien Thorn?" Margaret asked in a tremulous voice.

"Yes, and the others. You see, he's interested

in the relationship between the enormous power and influence they had on the one hand and the strain of tragedy that—"

"Don't talk to me about Damien Thorn." The words were delivered in a monotone as she wrung her hands together in her lap.

Anna felt suddenly cold and knew that all she could do was keep talking.

"Obviously if it upsets you, then I—"

Suddenly Margaret turned to face her. "You know nothing!" She was sneering now, getting to her feet, her hands outstretched, the half-inch nails looking like claws. Anna backed off, frightened and reached for the door.

Then, as soon as the fury had risen, it subsided. Margaret sat back down in the chair, covering her face with her hands as her shoulders heaved under the sobs.

Anna hovered, wondering what to do, wanting to comfort her but fearful of those terrible nails. For a full minute she stood undecided, then Margaret looked up and wiped her nose like a child with the back of her sleeve, and when the words came, they were said in the voice of a child.

"Sit down and I will tell you a story," she said. Anna nodded and sat primly on the bed, ready to spring for the door if necessary.

Then she remembered something and reached into her bag.

"Do you mind?" she asked as she pulled out a

tape recorder, but Margaret ignored it. It was as if she were talking to herself.

"It was the night of Armageddon," she began in a flat voice. . . .

Anna had never encountered insanity. Part of her wanted to leave, to save her time, but there was another part of her that was reluctantly fascinated. It was the same story. More Antichrists and Armageddons.

She let the woman ramble, thinking maybe it would help. Maybe the interview would be therapeutic.

Silence for a moment, then Margaret smiled.

"My husband was the bravest man in the world. It was he who tried to destroy the Antichrist that night, and it was I who killed him."

The smile vanished, and she slumped in her seat.

"I see his face in my dreams. As I went to him, he looked up at me, expecting me to save him. He had been mauled by the dog, you know. I can still see the look of surprise as I brought the knife down. That is the only consolation. In his last moment, he had no time for fear. Just surprise."

"But why?" The question escaped involuntarily, and Anna was instantly angry with herself for going along with this insane delusion.

"Because I was mad then," Margaret said softly. "You think I am mad now, but this is nothing. I had given myself to Satan."

Anne coughed, trying to hide the snort of contempt as Margaret moved forward, holding out
her hand, bending each finger into the palm
until only the index finger remained upright.

"The fire did not erase it" Margaret said.
"Look at the soft part." Anne squinted and saw
a small scar, a series of tiny curls that looked
like numbers, nines or sixes.

" 'Let he who hath understanding,' " said
Margaret. " 'reckon the number of the beast; for
it is a human number. . . .' "

Anna looked at it, and a fragmented memory
rose to her mind from her childhood.

"It's number is six hundred and sixty-six,"
she responded.

Margaret smiled triumphantly. "You see," she
said. Then the smile vanished, to be replaced by
a grimace of disgust. She rubbed her finger.
"The mark of the Beast," she repeated. "My
reward after my initiation." She articulated the
words carefully. "After I had lain with the devil's
disciple."

Anna had heard enough. She got to her feet,
trying to look and sound businesslike. She just
wanted to get away, but as she reached for the
tape recorder, Margaret got to her feet, arms
wrapped protectively around her chest.

"Aren't you going to ask me who it was?" she
asked in a girlish voice, striving to be coy.

Anna shook her head. "I don't think it's any of
my—"

"Paul Buher," she said. "You know him. I lay with him." She stepped forward, reaching out for Anna, trying to clutch her in an embrace. Her breath was foul, and Anna stood back, fumbling for the doorknob. "I was seduced by evil," Margaret whispered, "impregnated by evil."

Anna gagged and pulled at the doorknob. "Please, Mrs. Brennan," she pleaded, and Margaret stepped back, smiling like a gargoyle.

"And I would have given birth like that poor woman who lay with Damien. I would have produced an abomination like the one who stalks Pereford today."

The door was jammed, and Anna tugged at it, trying to look away, but somehow mesmerized by Margaret's gaze.

"But I defeated them. I destroyed the spawn of Satan as it slept in my womb." Without warning she took a step back, bent, and lifted her skirt with both hands, drawing it up to her stomach. Anne felt the scream build in her throat as she saw the terrible scars gouged out of her thighs, a delta of desecration, then she dragged her eyes away and turned to the door.

"And I saw the woman drunken with the blood of the saints," Margaret shouted, "and with the blood of the martyrs of Jesus!"

Anna tugged at the door and stumbled through as it creaked open.

"Purged by the bleach," Margaret shouted after her. "The abomination destroyed even as it slept!"

And then Anna was out in the corridor, slamming the door behind her, the force of her run smashing her into the opposite wall, hurting herself, holding one hand out to save herself, the tape recorder strapped around her wrist smacking against the tiles.

There was a strange chorus as the tape recorder burst into life, Margaret's voice booming along the corridor.

"Because I was mad then. You think I am mad now ..." While behind her the muffled voice seeped through the door. "These are the days of Tribulation when all things that have been prophesied will come to pass."

Anna snapped the machine off and turned to feel a hand on her shoulder. It was the young nun with the brown eyes.

"You will follow me."

Anna nodded and followed her quickly, hearing Margaret Brennan ranting at her from her cell. Her mind was a jumbled mess of emotions, and she knew only one thing: She would never be so glad to see fresh air and people who talked of nothing more exciting than the weather.

They turned into another corridor, and she blinked, wondering where they were going.

The nun stopped and opened a door. "If you wouldn't mind," she said, "the mother superior would like a quick word with you."

Anna hesitated. It was the last thing she wanted. But if the mother superior wanted to see her, then she would have to be accommodated. After all, she was a visitor in the place.

"Very well," she replied, "but only for a moment."

The nun smiled and stood back to let her enter. Anna walked into the room, and the nun gestured toward a chair by a table, then backed out and closed the door behind her.

Anna sighed and sat down, her legs trembling, then closed her eyes. She had a headache and her knees were weak. Slowly she took a dozen deep breaths until she felt herself calming down. Her heart stopped thumping wildly and her pulse returned to normal.

She opened her eyes and looked around her. The first thing she noticed was that the window was barred. She frowned and turned, gazing around the room. It was no bigger than Margaret's cell, and the walls were padded. Again she frowned. Just a small bed, a table, and one chair. Why *one* chair, if she was going to talk to the mother superior?

She went to the door, which had the same padding as the walls, then looked for the handle. There was none. Her heart began to pound again, and her throat was dry. She began knocking on the door, but it was like punching pillows.

"Excuse me," she shouted, but her voice was a squeak. She spoke again, louder this time.

Suddenly, with a clang, a grille was pulled open in the door, and she could see the little nun looking at her.

"May I see the mother superior now?" Anna asked as calmly as she could, hoping her voice did not tremble. The nun did not react, just turned and walked away, while Anna yelled at her to come back.

Anna whimpered, her fingers digging into the grille. She tried to tell herself that this was just a silly mistake, that maybe the nuns were vowed to silence and the little one was just going for the mother superior. Then two others came into view, walking along the corridor, arm in arm. As they came closer, Anna noticed that the crucifixes around their necks looked strange, but it wasn't until they were standing only a foot away, looking at her, that she saw the figures on the gold chains; identical figures; gargoyle mouths, the chests of bulls, cloven hooves, and monstrous phalluses.

When she screamed, one of the nuns reached up and snapped the grille shut.

She screamed for an hour, until she was hoarse, her screams soaking into the mattresses, her fists beating a silent drumbeat on the door. Then Anna began to cry, her sobs unheard by everyone except herself.

PART THREE

⊷§ CHAPTER 10 §⊷

SINCE CHILDHOOD JACK Mason had loved flying, whether it was the latest transatlantic Concorde or a two-seater hopping among the Caribbean islands. He had never felt the tiniest tremor of apprehension—until now.

As flight PA 100 from Kennedy Airport circled above London Heathrow, he clutched the armrest and fought to stop the trembling. The woman next to him was looking at him, his anxiety infecting her; if this great bear of a man was frightened, then maybe there was good reason.

It was the thought of the little man smeared on the wheel that wouldn't let go no matter how hard Mason tried to banish the image; that, and the memory of his wife's face. His bladder ached, but he did not dare get out of his seat in case he found himself somewhere he shouldn't be. And so, yet again, he reached into his briefcase and went over Anna's notes, although he virtually knew them by heart; anything to act as a diversion.

He ran his finger down the list and stopped at the name of Carol Wyatt, then checked Anna's notes. The young journalist had been found in a shallow grave, and the inquest mentioned teeth marks on her ankle and the back of her neck. Her body had been found a couple of weeks after she had disappeared. Her last article had been about a series of deaths known as the Crucifixion Killings, inexplicable murders commited by daggers whose hilts had been fashioned in the shape of Christ on the cross.

Anna had written that she was going to check the story out with one of Carol's colleagues, a political analyst named James Richard.

Mason grunted to himself. Daggers, shallow graves, teethmarks. It was all getting very complicated, but as he tried to make some sense of it, the flight attendants voice came over the intercom, telling the passengers to fasten their seat belts for landing.

For the next three and a half minutes Mason forgot all about Philip Brennan, Paul Buher, and Damien Thorn. His eyes were closed, and for the first time since he had renounced his faith, he prayed to a God he no longer recognized for a safe landing. It was not until they had taxied to the terminal gate that he opened his eyes, feeling a mixture of relief and shame that he had been such a hypocrite.

He was through customs and immigration in record time. People did not fly so much anymore, not since the climatic changes and the dangers of unexpected turbulence. At the arrivals lounge he stopped and looked around expectantly, but Anna wasn't there. He was disappointed. She hadn't promised to meet him, but he'd thought she would turn up. Anna was a nice mixture of professionalism and sentimentality, the sort who would drop everything to meet someone at an airport, but evidently not this time.

He checked the message board. Nothing. "Welcome to London," he muttered aloud and saw the woman who had sat next to him looking at him again, this time in pity. He winked at her and headed for the cab stand.

He had booked into a small expensive hotel in South Kensington, popular with movie people who wanted anonymity. It was discreetly luxurious, the staff were paid enough not to tip off the gossip writers. He wouldn't be pestered.

The owner was abroad, and there was no one he knew in the place. When he was unpacking, he felt suddenly and unreasonably lonely. He called Anna's number and got her machine, left a message, and headed for the shower.

When he came out, the phone was ringing. It was the front desk informing him that his word processor had arrived, ordered by Miss Brompton. Moments later a young man knocked at the door and wheeled the machine inside. Mason stepped back and stared at it. It was massive, a keyboard, monitor, and computer and a case full of accessories. It looked as if it could take him to the moon.

The technician began setting it up and explaining it to him.

"It's the very latest model, sir," he said. "Your assistant said you wanted the best."

Mason nodded and peered at it. He was reluctantly impressed. He was one of the old-fashioned kind who worked on an ancient portable typewriter and had always distrusted anything else, holding the superstitious belief that the gadgetry would somehow block the flow of inspiration.

"And this, sir." It was an envelope.

Mason opened it and saw a tiny cassette and a note from Anna saying that he might like to try it out on the machine. It was, she had written, her little joke.

He held it up and blinked at it, asked the technician what to do with it. The man slipped it into the cassette deck, hit a button, and stood back as the machine gurgled to life. Words began to stammer across the screen, green letters on a blue background.

The Revelation of Jesus Christ, which God gave unto Him, to show unto his servants things which must shortly come to pass.

Mason blinked. "What the hell is that?"

"If I remember rightly from my Sunday-school days, it's the first verse of the Book of Revelation, the last book of the Bible."

"Christ," said Mason.

The young man was squinting at the tape and nodding. "Yes, it's marked on the packet." He turned and beamed. "You can get all the books of the Bible from the shop sir. Both Testaments. I've seen their brochure. And the complete works of Shakespeare."

"Any of mine?"

"I'm sorry sir, I didn't notice, but I expect so. Just about everything ever written has been processed."

"Christ," said Mason again, staring at the machine as the words continued to chase themselves across the screen.

Blessed is he that readeth, and they that hear the words of this prophecy, and keep those things which are written therein: for the time is at hand.

He shook his head, then began to play with the computer, wondering what Anna was thinking of, sending him such a strange tape to practice on. He hoped she wasn't starting to crack under the pressure.

For two days Mason deluded himself that he was mixing business with pleasure. He had lunch with his publisher one day, then with his London agent the next. He looked up an old friend and they hit a few bars together. On the third day he woke feeling guilty.

There was no business mixed with the pleasure. He had simply been enjoying himself.

For the sixth time he tried Anna's number, but only the machine answered. There was no message to tell him where she was or when she would be back.

He would just have to work on his own until she turned up. It was annoying, but there was nothing he could do about it. First he bought a roll of paper, spread it on the floor, and wrote the names of each member of the family in various colors of ink, working out a rough chronology. That done, he wrote each name on Anna's list on a separate piece of paper and taped both pieces to the wall.

All dead. Only Damien Thorn had died a natural death, and that in itself was strange. How could a thirty-two-year-old man suddenly drop with a heart attack when he had apparently been in perfect health? Damien had never been ill, Anne had said, not even measles as a child, and that itself was odd.

He stood back and gazed at the names. Carol Wyatt. That was the one to go for. Maybe Anna had already spoken to her contact in Fleet Street; maybe the man knew where she was. It was worth a try, anyway. He phoned the newspaper and a sniffy female voice said that Mr. Richard was not available. Who was calling? Mason gave his name and one line of description. The answer came back breathlessly, and Mason grinned. A couple of Pulitzers worked wonders on secretaries.

Within ten minutes Richard had been found and was on the line saying he would be delighted to have lunch at Mason's hotel.

He arrived an hour later, a tall man, elegantly dressed as befitted someone who mingled with the powers-that-be on a first-name basis, and so experienced in the ways of diplomacy that his advice was sought regularly.

Ministers had come and gone, but James Richard was a Whitehall fixture.

At first, over lunch, they talked politics. Richard reminiscing about the British initiative that had failed a year earlier. The Foreign Secretary had arranged a Summit conference in London that had ended in fiasco and led directly to the war known as Armageddon.

"What ever became of him?" Mason asked.

"Fishing, I should imagine, probably terminally," responded Richard. "He was something of a fool. Eton, Oxford, and wine bars, if you know what I mean."

Mason didn't, but he allowed the small talk to continue for the required amount of time. He knew from experience that people like Richard expected the formalities to be observed.

He gave it ten minutes, then put the question to the man.

"Anna Brompton was in touch?"

"Yes, she called, but then nothing."

Mason nodded. "She's gone out of town for a while, which is why I'm grateful to you for coming."

Richard smiled, laced his fingers, and asked how he could help, and Mason told him. At the mention of the name Carol Wyatt, he frowned.

"A tragedy," he said. "Dreadful business."

"Bit of a mystery, isn't it?" Mason said. "No one caught, no motive?"

Richard shrugged. "She came to see me, you know, a few days before she disappeared. Wanted my help on a story, some nonsense about daggers, wanted to get hold of the American ambassador." He smiled to himself and shook his head. "Silly girl."

Now Mason was interested, and asked what the connection was between Brennan and the daggers.

Again Richard shrugged. "Sorry," he said, "this is wasting your time, but she heard that I'd spoken to Brennan in Rome. He'd been given a dagger by some crazy monk, some lunatic raving about the devil walking the land or something. Carol seemed to take it seriously. She was young, after all, not very experienced."

Suddenly Mason snapped his fingers. "Add two and two and you get eight," he said.

"Pardon?"

Mason grinned. "Nothing," he said. "I just made a crazy connection. False logic. Sorry."

The conversation returned to politics, but Mason couldn't concentrate. He kept thinking of Brennan and the place where Carol's body was found. A ditch in Berkshire. Pereford was in Berkshire. Somehow, wherever he looked, he was always brought back to the place.

Pereford. The name was beginning to haunt him, and he had to struggle to keep the conversation alive.

". . . busy week ahead," Richard was saying. "I've got the Summit conference in Rome and the damned Bilderberg at the same time."

Mason nodded. The Bilderberg Club was another subject he had considered investigating. All those financiers and politicians meeting annually to sort out the destiny of the world, always in complete secrecy. It was unofficial, so it was said; just a meeting of like-minded friends, and therefore accountable to no one. There were no electors to worry about, or shareholders, and so there were no communiqués, no memos, and certainly no reporters.

What made Mason's antennae twitch was Richard's next remark, that the chairman of the conference this year was to be Bill Jeffries of the Thorn Corporation.

"Does that mean that the young Thorn will be going?" he asked.

Richard shook his head. "I don't know. He's an enigma, that young man, as approachable as Howard Hughes."

"As Howard Hughes *was*."

"No. I meant what I said the first time."

Mason grinned, and Richard preened, enjoying his little joke. "Do you think you could do me a favor?" Mason asked. "Could you get hold of Jeffries for me, tell him I want to meet him?"

Richard shook his head. "Sorry, old man, out of the question. No one gets near that conference. Not even I."

"But you could try, couldn't you?"

Now it was Richard's antennae that twitched. In his world no one did anything for nothing. Favors had to be repaid.

"I'll certainly make the effort for you, Mr. Mason."

"Jack."

"Jack. And perhaps one day you might consider giving an interview to my paper."

Mason frowned. He hadn't talked to the papers for years, believing that his work spoke for him and any attempts to explain it would be unnecessary and self-defeating. Nor did he think that his personal life was anyone's business.

"My editor would be honored," Richard continued.

"Would you do the interview?" Mason asked.

Richard shook his head. "I would be delighted, of course, but I'm afraid we're very departmentalized. There are lines of demarcation, and I'm strictly political."

Mason sighed, then nodded in agreement. It would have to be done. If anyone could get near Jeffries it would be Richard. "Okay," he said. "But get somebody good. I don't want some hack who'll make things up."

"On *my* paper?" Richard said in mock reproach. Then the two men shook hands and Richard was gone, leaving Mason to wonder if he'd done the right thing.

❧ CHAPTER II ❧

A THORN IN HIS SIDE

"CHRIST," MASON GROANED when he opened the paper. The interview had been given the
full treatment, a center spread, two full pages,
with a six-column picture of him, feet up beside
the word processor, a bourbon in his hand.

As he read, he swore constantly, using up all
the words, and some he thought he had forgotten.
It wasn't that the woman had misquoted him, it
was her style—so damned coy. But she had also
picked up on something he had said about the
Thorn virus being almost paranormal and had
made the most of it. What was worse, she had
printed the name of the hotel. Before he'd
finished, the phone started ringing off the wall.

By evening he thought he would start screaming. The interview might have been useful if there had been some sort of screening process to deal with the calls it had produced and if Anna had been around to weed out the crazies from the genuine. As it was, he was captured. The whole country knew he was in town with his Pulitzers under his belt and, it was implied, a six-figure advance to spend on research, which meant that every charlatan and his mother could spot a grubsteak. And yet he couldn't afford to turn them away in case just one of them was genuine.

By the third day he was near breaking point, sick of all those who claimed to know about the Thorns, sick of women who claimed to be witches, of gypsies who claimed to have witnessed the Second Coming. And the hotel staff were getting annoyed, discreetly annoyed but annoyed nonetheless.

He had decided to move to another hotel when the phone rang again. It was a voice he knew well, the young man from the front desk.

"A gentleman to see you, sir."

"Who now?"

"A butler, sir."

"Huh?"

"He says he's from a place called Pereford, sir."

Mason blinked, asked him to send the man

135

up. There had been no mention of Pereford in the article, so maybe this was genuine.

A knock at the door and then Mason was staring down into an old face, pink and bald. He was reminded of a Victorian doll, something dug out of an attic.

He stood back to let the old man in, heard the squeaky voice introduce itself as George. Just George.

"Thank you for coming, George," he said, indicating a chair. "But at the risk of being rude, have you any identification?"

George reached into his pocket, and for some reason Mason felt the need to elaborate. "It's just that there's been so many impostors—"

He stopped talking as he found himself looking at a photograph of Damien Thorn with George standing behind him, a younger George, but definitely George, and most definitely Damien Thorn.

"Taken eighteen years ago, sir," the old man said, "by a camera crew, when they were making a film at Pereford. Miss Reynolds, you know."

"Kate Reynolds?"

"Quite, sir."

Mason fought to contain his enthusiasm. After all these charlatans, here was the real thing. He gestured to a chair, but George had wandered across to the office and was staring at the charts.

"Have I got it right?" asked Mason.

George nodded, then turned. "I have come

136

here for two things, Mr. Mason. First to warn, second to confess."

Mason shrugged and saw George looking at the liquor cabinet. It was to be scotch. Mason poured a large one and watched the old man gulp it greedily.

"I am not a drinker sir," George said, "It's for my heart. It needs stimulation. Temporary stimulation, that is." George tried a smile which turned into a grimace. He sat down, his hands shaking, then looked up at Mason.

"Are you a religious man, sir?"

"No." Mason groaned inwardly. Not more damned nonsense. He had had enough. "Look, let's get one thing clear, George," he said, but the old man held up his hand for silence.

"Please hear me out. It is better that you are not religious. You can think about this in a detached way." He took a notebook from his pocket and laid it on the table. "It is all in here. I have made notes for you."

Mason flopped down next to him, suppressing a yawn. He would listen to the old man, then he would move to another hotel. He could not take any more of this hokum.

"I don't expect you to believe at first," George was saying, "but you'll know, of course, that the Bible says: after Armageddon the Millennium."

"Of course," said Mason wearily.

"But there's no sign of peace, is there?"

Mason shook his head.

"In this notebook, I have shown you why. Read the twenty-second book of the New Testament. Chapter three, verse eight. Then read the interpretations. Then check back. You will find the link." He raised one hand. " 'And Satan shall be loosed out of his prison and shall go out to deceive the nations which are in the four corners of the earth, Gog and Magog, to gather them together to do battle: the number of whom is as the sand of the sea.' "

Mason nodded. "You said you were here to warn me."

"Forget the Thorns, Mr. Mason. You know not what you do."

"You mean, there are more things in heaven and earth—"

"Exactly," George said. "Shakespeare got it right. Leave them alone or you shall perish."

Mason had had enough. "Okay, that's the warning. Now the confession."

"Thank you." George got to his feet and looked down at him. "I am making use of you, Mr. Mason. I have tried to pray to Christ. He has appeared to me in dreams, but I cannot do it. No sooner do I try than I tremble. I have palpitations. The words literally stick in my throat. On the way here I tried to enter a church and I fainted. I could not step upon hallowed ground because of this."

Mason squinted at the finger thrust in front of him, the tiny scab, three curls.

"The mark of the Beast, Mr. Mason. It's all in the notebook."

Mason sighed and shook his head. "Are you nearly finished?"

"Yes. In more ways than one. I was told once that my soul was safely damned, and I fear it is true. However, by warning you and confessing to you, I hope I may have redeemed myself." He turned toward the door. "Now I am dead," he said softly. "He will know I have betrayed him. There are no secrets. I can only hope I have repented in time."

Mason went to the door and opened it. When they shook hands Mason shuddered. George's hand was cold and clammy, as if the blood had been drained from his body and the man was already dead. He looked into the old face, and the eyes that gazed dully back at him were reminiscent of the open-eyed stare of a corpse.

"You say you are not a religious man, Mr. Mason, but I would be grateful if you would pray for me. It would not do you any harm and it just might do me some good. Would you?"

"Yes." Mason was surprised to find himself agreeing. It was like giving a dollar to a derelict; it meant little to him but a lot to the derelict. George squeezed his hand once more and made his way unsteadily through the door.

"Just one thing," said Mason. "Have you heard the name Anna Brompton?"

George shook his head.

"She was working for me, and she's disappeared."

George smiled. "Of course she has. So will you. No one survives." He moved unsteadily down the corridor, then paused and turned back. "Thank you for the whisky, Mr. Mason. It may just get me home."

Mason nodded, then closed the door and moved to the window to look down into the street. A moment later the old man emerged, clutching his coat around him, bending low as if walking into a gale. The trees were motionless. Only the old man was caught in the eye of some hurricane, his coat flapping at his knees as he turned the corner and vanished. Mason knew that he would never see him again.

It took George nearly an hour to find a taxi that would take him all the way to Pereford.

On the way back he thought of Mason. The man's courtesy had not hidden his skepticism. He would not believe, but at least George knew that he had made the effort, there was no more he could do.

As he approached the place where his soul was kept captive, he felt weaker. He might move physically away from the place, but his soul was held in hock until he returned—and for most of his life George had taken comfort in that thought.

It was dark by the time the cab reached the

house. George eased himself out and handed over a wad of money.

"I don't need it any more," he said in answer to the driver's astonished burble of thanks, then he slowly made his way through the lodge gate and up the drive.

The driver watched him go. Cancer, he thought. The old man smelled of death. He looked down at the tip he had been given and then did something completely out of character. He threw the notes out the window and hit the accelerator, glad to be away from the place.

George felt his heart lurch as he walked up the drive. The wind had died, and he could see bright eyes looking at him from the hedgerow, the stoats and the rabbits; it was time for their nightly dance of death.

The whisky had left a sour taste, and he felt bile rise in his throat. As he turned the last corner he saw that the house was dark. Damien would be in his chapel. It was his time, the hour when he went to pray to renew his spiritual strength. George turned and looked up the hill through the trees to the old church, the white-wash bright against the black sky.

"Please God," he said, but, as he spoke, the bile rose in his throat and choked him so that the word "God" came out as a strangled grunt. He spat in disgust and blood glistened on the lawn.

The thought of eternity terrified him. Now

that it was near, the specters of his childhood rose to sabotage his peace of mind; his brain worked against him, resurrecting stories of eternal hellfire. Images of the Inferno danced in front of him, nightmares of monsters with toasting forks, speared bodies writhing in the flames. All the stories that he had dismissed as superstitious nonsense he now saw for real in the bloodstains on the ground as he coughed and spluttered his way up the hill.

He had no feeling now in his left arm. The pains that had coursed through his chest and down to his fingertips had gone, and now there was nothing: a dead limb. George tried to flex his fingers but could not move them. He would rather have the pain, for the agony was better than this terrible nothingness.

His vision blurred as strange ripples moved across his left eye and he bumped against the curb. Then whole areas of his vision blanked out and he had to concentrate hard, closing one eye and staring straight ahead.

He did not notice Damien standing by the treeline, and his first realization that he was not alone was the growling of the dog.

He stopped, turned, and peered at them. Damien was smiling at him; the dog was tense, ready to spring.

He raised his right hand to his brow, shading his good eye to see better. At the sudden movement, the dog twitched and bared its teeth, the huge head level with the old man's chest, and George knew that it could cover the few yards between them in one leap.

"He is thinking of ending your life here and now," said Damien. "On the very spot where you gave him birth." He smiled, teeth glinting. "There's gratitude for you, George."

The old man tried to speak, but there was nothing to be said, no defense against what he had done, no mitigation.

"So, old man," Damien continued, speaking softly. "Do you think the Nazarene will save you now?"

George shook his head. "Forgive me," he said. "Please."

"No," said Damien, his smile replaced by a scowl. "My father does not forgive. I do not forgive. You have the wrong one." He shook his head, his voice a sneer of sarcasm. "It is strange, is it not? You, who brought me the message from my father that the thousand years is but one day, you turn from me, renouncing me, my father and my father's father, and dare to ask forgiveness."

He stepped back and pointed toward the church.

"There is your straight and narrow path," he said, "all ten yards of it. Go on, old man. Go meet your Maker, if you can."

A sob racked George's chest, and a trickle of

blood ran down his chin as he hobbled past Damien. He could not look at him.

The dog grunted, and for a moment George thought it was going to spring, but it was only stalking him, moving a yard behind him while the taunts of its master followed him.

"Don't you think you are a little late, George? Don't you think that you are being presumptuous to expect redemption at the last hour? Do you expect the Nazarene to be so easily fooled? He is, after all, your Maker. He knows you. He knows that it is fear, not love of Him, and that won't do, George. It is not enough."

Slowly, dragging one foot after another, George reached the door and pushed it open, looking up through the shattered roof before turning to glance behind him. Damien and the dog stood framed in the gateway, unable to follow him. They were silent now. The dog's ears were flat against its head, the lips drawn back in a silent snarl. Damien was motionless, looking at him curiously, and, for a moment the old man thought he saw a glimpse of pity on the young face, and perhaps regret; and he remembered what he had once thought, that Damien had not asked for his destiny.

Again he turned and made his way up the nave, feeling only sorrow for the young man, a measure of compassion that he recognized as being Christian sympathy; then he noticed something that made him want to cry with relief. His left arm was tingling with pins and needles, coming alive again, the blood pumping through the old veins, and he gave a silent prayer of thanks.

It seemed to take him forever to reach the altar. There were no pews to grab for support and the nave was a rutted track, but at least his vision had cleared and he could see perfectly. The pounding in his chest frightened him, but the nausea had gone and there was no longer any blood on his chin.

He stopped at the altar and gazed at the crucifix, wondering how Buher had managed to do the job. The figure of Christ was securely lashed to the crossbeam, and as he stared up at the face, it seemed to be beckoning to him. The eyes held his gaze so that he could almost imagine that it was Christ Himself soothing him, suffering him to come to Him.

The ladder was propped against the joist, the top rung level with the head. George reached for it, grasped the nearest rung, and looked up.

"Forgive me, Lord, for a lifetime of sin."

A high-pitched cackle behind him made him shudder. He turned to see Damien still by the gate, and he shivered, thinking of scavengers, of jackals and hyenas, of creatures waiting for him to die. Again Damien was taunting him, yelling at him to go and meet his Maker.

Taunted from behind, encouraged from above,

George placed one foot on the ladder and dragged the other behind it, panting with the effort.

Every movement caused him to gasp and his heart to batter against his ribs, and he had to stop on each rung to rest until he was ready to take the next step.

His palms were wet with perspiration and slipped as he reached up. He felt a splinter of wood gouge through the index finger of his left hand, and again he gave thanks for the pain. The pounding of his heart was getting worse.

Still Damien taunted him while George told himself not to look down. He was tempted to turn, but he knew that if he did, he would fall.

His strength was seeping out of him now, and he pressed his face and his body hard against the ladder. The wood against his cheek reminded him of the Crucifixion, the unbearable thought of nails being pounded through hands and feet and the wonder that human beings could even think of such things; but the idea had not come from any man. It had been conceived by the dark power, the force of evil, something he knew well.

"Forgive me," he said again and heard the answering mockery behind him.

"Forgive him, Nazarene! Take him to Your bosom if you feel he is worthy of You!"

George dragged himself up another rung, then another. He was level with the charred limbs, his face inches from the loincloth, and he could hear Damien laughing again, and for a moment he thought he could go no farther. There was no strength left in him, but he could not go down and he could not stay motionless.

"Lord give me strength," he whispered. There was an itch at the base of his skull, where the mark of the Beast had appeared all those years ago, the three tiny sixes. He had been proud that day, and now he was being mocked, the mark demanding to be scratched when he could not move his hand to relieve it.

With the last effort of his will he heaved himself up the final two rungs until he was looking into the face of Christ, and he thought of the madman named Yigael who had carved it—a labor of insanity, the last thing he had done before killing himself.

He could see the daggers embedded in the spine and the six-inch nails that made the crown of thorns, and he remembered that terrible night when Damien had carried it from the black chapel, when the nails had slipped and gouged into his neck.

"I am here to ask forgiveness, Lord, not of a graven image but of what it represents. I have wasted my life. You have come to me at the end in dreams, seeking my soul, offering redemption, and now I ask for it, for You to take me into Your Father's Kingdom as You have promised."

A shriek of abuse made him turn, and he stared at the figure of Damien by the gate. Yellow eyes pierced his soul with that look of command that George had seen in the eyes of the boy's father, demanding obedience.

As his feet started to slip, he turned and looked into the face of Christ. He fell, but only an inch. The crown of thorns ripped into his eyes, holding him suspended for a fraction of time, and in that moment George knew the agony of the Crucifixion. Then the nails tore through the eyesockets and released him.

Arms outstretched, tailcoat flapping, he fell, the scream dying instantly when he smashed onto the altar and slithered to the ground. Then there was silence, except for the drip of the blood falling from the face of Christ onto the altar.

And before the dust settled, his soul had fled from his body.

❧ CHAPTER 12 ❧

JACK MASON WAS worried. He had moved to the Hilton and was no longer being pestered. Now he had time to think, and what he thought bothered him. His story was not coming together. All he had was a crowd of pop-eyed fundamentalists raving about the Book of Revelation. He knew the point of Anna's little joke now, but he was not laughing. He was sick to death of the goddam Book of Revelation and he was no closer to the Thorns than he had been when he started.

He had set up the word processor in the sitting room and, after transcribing the old man's notes, sat feeding them into the machine. It was an essay in madness, and he cursed as he hit the keys, watching the words come up on the screen:

Damien Thorn, conceived of a union
between Satan and a jackal and born in
a hospital in Rome, the biblical Babylon.

"A jackal," he grunted. "Oh, for Chrissake."

The son was excreted into the world,
conceived through sodomy.
"Check his body," George had written.
"There is no navel, for there was no
umbilical cord."

"Jesus," Mason said. Tapping out the name
Carol Wyatt, he studied the response on the
screen. She had made the fatal mistake of exposing the young man's weakness. He had been the
victim of an attack of lust combined with affec-
tion, and so she had to die, so that his soul
would be cleansed of this aberration.

It was madness, of course, but it made a kind
of insane logic. Ignore the Satanic nonsense,
Mason told himself, and you've got some kind of
evil at work, attracting people toward it before
disposing of them.

Then there were all the biblical references
and the final message from the old man that the
mortal remains of Damien Thorn were not in
the mausoleum in Chicago but at Pereford, where
the son drew spiritual strength from them.

As he looked at the screen, a flash of memory
came to him: the fat barman telling him about
the little priest. Mason grunted and shook his

head. Insane logic, a contradiction in terms: but what to do about it?

Maybe his agent had been right after all.

The phone rang. At first Mason was tempted to ignore it, but he picked it up and snarled out his room number.

"Hi!" A bright voice, female.

"Who's this?"

"Your researcher. I'm in the bar."

Mason saw himself in the mirror. He was beaming.

"What researcher? Which bar?"

"How many have you got?" said Anna. "And it's the bar on the right as you come in, not the basement full of Filipinos."

Mason laughed, told her to drop her drink and come up.

She looked different somehow; slimmer, maybe sexier. Their relationship had always been strictly professional, but when he kissed her, she squirmed like a hooker.

"Okay," he said, "tell me."

"I don't know," she said. "I got amnesia. One minute I'm happily working for you, the next I'm in a police station in Highgate with no memory. I've lost a week of my life." Her cheerfulness failed her, and she frowned, shrugged her shoulders, and flapped her hand in front of her face as if swatting an invisible fly.

He held her close, stroking her hair, until she

had recovered. When they broke apart, her smile was back in place.

"I want to carry on," she said.

"I don't know," said Mason. "You were right about the story in your last phone call. I had it translated into English—it's a crock of crap."

"Are you giving up?"

He shook his head. "Not until we've covered every angle. I'll give it another month. If there's nothing then, I'll call it quits."

"Okay." She was chirpy again, ready to go to work, asking him what he'd discovered while she was on her memory vacation. He told her, showed her the charts, told her about George, then held out his hand. "Have you brought the package?" he asked.

"What package?"

"In your last message you mentioned a package from the Italian."

She frowned, wrinkling her brow.

"Part of the amnesia?" he asked.

"Must be."

"Do you think it will come back?"

"I hope so. The doctor seems to think so."

She turned and walked away. Mason was about to ask her more but decided against it. Better leave it to the medical people. The best thing was to keep her occupied.

"Okay," he said. "I'll give you a choice. An astronomer in Sussex or a trip to Rome with your friend James Richard."

Anna mimed the tossing of a coin.

"Rome."

"I thought you'd say that." They kissed again, and Mason wondered if it was his imagination, or if her amnesia was making her horny. He tossed his own mental coin and decided that it was his imagination. It had to be. The one golden rule in his business was that you don't go around screwing your assistant.

Driving to Sussex that night, Mason tried to put the book out of his mind. He was going to take a vacation from it and enjoy himself. The astronomer's letter was an oasis of sense in a desert of religious claptrap.

"I read the article about you," the man had written, "and would like to invite you to my observatory. You may be interested in something known as the Trinity alignment, a movement in the galaxies some eighteen years ago. It has no rational link with your book, but I have some material on the Thorns. All it needs from you is to suspend your sense of the absurd for a time."

And the address: Fernbank Observatory on the Sussex Downs. The man sounded sane. It would make a nice change, even if the trip was of no consequence.

Mason was on time when he reached the small

domed building dominated by a massive reception bowl. As he got out, he checked the sky. For once there were a few gaps in the clouds. At the very least, there would be stars to look at.

Barry King had heard him coming and was waiting at the door. A small man, with a slight stammer and as nervous as a sparrow, he thanked Mason for coming, said he'd read some of his books and they were a lot better than the films they had made from them. For a moment Mason thought the man was going to ask him for his autograph, but he just smiled and ushered him up the spiral staircase to the dome.

For ten minutes King showed him around, proud of the round room, the bank of monitors, the computer, the library of prints that made up his atlas of the cosmos. Mason was impressed. For half an hour he asked questions that helped put the little man at ease.

King had been apprehensive about inviting him in case he was wasting his time, but Mason was obviously interested. He didn't say "Is that so?" or anything like that, the way some people did. His eyes didn't glaze over. And when he was offered the chance to look through the microscope, he took it with all the enthusiasm of a boy.

"The constellation of Orion," King said, hitting a button. Mason stepped back and looked down as a photograph of the area he'd just been gazing at slid out of a chute beneath the microscope. King took it to a light box and spread it on the glass. The stars blinked at him.

"We can blow it up, focus in. We can see into the very depths of the universe."

He slipped the print into a folder, then picked up a file marked Trinity.

"The reason I asked you to come," said King.

"It happened eighteen years ago," he said, "and I still can't understand it." The prints were meaningless to Mason at first. Three blimps changing position, closing in on one another.

"An alignment," explained King. "I was just the assisant at the time. A man called John Favell was the astronomer. He died three years ago, poor chap. He found the movement in the region known as Cassiopeia. Three stars moving into an alignment. Impossible, of course. And this is why I asked you to come, after reading that article."

Mason did not understand, and it took a long time for King to explain; Favell had been contacted by a priest, some nonsense about the Second Coming of Christ, the movement in the heavens predicted centuries earlier.

"Like the star of Bethlehem?" Mason asked.

"Exactly. Hokum, of course, but Mr. Favell was a tolerant man. He let the priest and two monks come and see the alignment, tried to joke with them, told him that he saw only the sky through his telescope and not the heavens, which I thought was a nice line, but they didn't seem to get it. They actually cried when it happened. I'll never forget their faces, three men filled with religious wonder. It's an astonishing thing, the power of faith. I truly wish I had it."

Always religion, Mason thought. This story always comes back to religion.

"Mr. Favell wrote a paper about it. He called it the Trinity alignment, but of course the priest had to call it the Holy Trinity." He smiled and shrugged as he stacked the prints. "We found the point of maximum intensity, a simple piece of mathematics, projecting it onto the earth's surface. It wasn't far from here."

He reached into his desk and produced a folder, flipped it open, and thumbed through a pile of letters.

"The priest corresponded with us after that night. It's a remarkable story of madness, how he and the monks went to the spot and witnessed the Second Coming of Christ."

"When was all this?"

"March twenty-fourth, 'eighty-two."

"When I saw the article in the paper," King said, "I was reminded of these letters."

Mason looked expectantly at him, knowing what he was going to hear and wondering what the connection was.

King pointed to a paragraph. " 'Remember, Mr. Favell,' " Mason read aloud, "that Damien Thorn is the Antichrist and—' " Mason swore violently, and King grinned at him.

"There's just one more thing, Mr. Mason," he said, reaching for another letter that was clipped to a second set of prints.

"After Mr. Favell's paper was published, we received this from the Cape Hattie observatory. Another inexplicable movement that happened years earlier. The birth of a star. A black star."

But it wasn't the photograph that caught Mason's eye. It was the time slug at the top: 6-6-6.

King saw him look at it, thought he detected a shudder go through Mason. 'Six a.m. on the sixth of June,' King explained. "The priest got excited when we told him. Made a mental leap of colossal presumption. It was the birthday of Damien Thorn. And three sixes is—"

"I know," said Mason. "The mark of the Beast."

For a moment, the briefest second, Mason felt a tremor of fear as his skepticism shattered. Then the fear turned to anger. His reason battered the superstition from his mind and he swore again, then looked into King's face.

"It's nonsense, all this, isn't it?" he asked. It was almost a plea.

"Of course," said King. "It must be. Nonsense. Coincidence." He shrugged. "It must be. Because if you believe otherwise then science is meaningless. Surely?"

The two men looked at each other and a tremor of doubt flowed between them, like electricity.

*   *   *

At Pereford Damien lay prostrate in his chapel beside the altar, weeping for the lost souls of George and Buher and for himself.

Now he had no one, and the loneliness was agony. He wept in self-pity, shaking his head and rubbing his knuckles into his eyes, knowing there was little time left. Then he got to his feet and gazed at the remains of his father. Gradually, the sorrow began to turn to anger, and he fought to conquer his weakness, to turn it into a terrible strength.

He closed his eyes and focused his mind on his destiny, calling up images of Christ and railing silently against them, the rage building in him until it burst into a stream of abuse. Fingers clenched, he roared his hatred of the benign influence of his enemy and screamed for vengeance, for the fallen angel, for his father and for himself, drawing strength from his rage and venting it against anyone who tried to fight against him.

In his car, heading back toward London, Jack Mason became conscious of a sudden chill and a stab of irrational panic. When he looked in his mirror, the face of an old, frightened man stared back at him.

❦ CHAPTER 13 ❧

JAMES RICHARD, AS he packed for the trip, was patiently trying to explain to his wife the reason why it was so important. But she couldn't grasp the significance.

"What do you mean, secret?" she asked. "Like the Freemasons?"

"Something like that," he replied. "Only multiply by a thousand." He turned and gave her his pacifying smile, the expression that summed up the failure of his marriage. He realized that he had grown past his wife years ago. Working with top politicians in the international corridors of power had given him insights into the way the world was run, while she would still watch *News at Ten* and comment on the hairstyle of the newcaster.

"Fifty years ago," he said, "the Bilderberg Club was formed as a club of politicians and businessmen with the interests of NATO at heart. Now it's much more than that. It has expanded to include the most powerful people in the East and the West. And in complete secrecy they sort out the world between them—for example, which country's debts is going to be called in, which war is going to be financed, which repressive little regime needs to be toppled. All so that the financial status quo remains the same and the power remains in the same hands."

"Ah," she said.

"It's the most exclusive closed shop in the world, and no one ever speaks. The security is colossal, the decisions are final, and there is no court of appeal. If the club decides, let us say, that Argentina is to be bankrupted, then there is nothing any Argentine can do about it, be he democrat or general."

"Do you think this is a good thing?" she asked.

"It creates global stability."

"But what about the losers?"

"There will always be losers, my dear."

"I suppose so," said Eva. "Well, never mind."

Richard sighed, pecked his wife on the cheek, and said he'd see her in a week. Even as he mouthed the words, he was thinking that Rome would be nice this year and full of people who knew which end was up.

*   *   *

As the aircraft banked for landing, the passengers on the port side nudged one another and stared down at the scene awaiting them. Leonardo da Vinci Airport was like an armed camp. From his seat in first class James Richard could see tanks on the approach roads, and a swarm of army helicopters buzzing beneath.

He had never seen such security. Never before had the Summit coincided with the Bilderberg, and as far as he knew, never before had so many world leaders gathered together at the same place. As the plane touched down, he thought about the man in charge of security and did not envy him one bit. It just needed one lunatic with one of those new nuclear devices that could fit into a small bag, and the world would be looking for a new set of leaders.

It was going to be a tough week. He had three men working with him on the Summit and one staking out the hotel six kilometers to the north where the Bilderberg was meeting. It would mean filing his copy twice a day, but at least Rome was ideal for communications. If only there was something to say.

On the way into the city his cab was held up in traffic. Richard idly gazed around him at a group of cripples, two on crutches, one in a wheelchair, and then a family, the man horribly scarred around the face as if he had been burned, the woman blind, with a white stick in one hand and a baby in her arms.

Then a third group, all moving in the one direction. He pointed them out to the driver and asked what was going on. The man shrugged.

"No one knows," he said. "They've been arriving for the last three days, in buses and trains. St. Peter's Square is full of them. Damned nuisance."

The traffic jam cleared slightly, and the cab slowly moved past the blind woman. Richard noticed that the baby was also scarred, as if it too had been in some terrible fire. He shuddered and turned his head away, feeling ill. He never could stand the sight of any deformity. Cripples made him sick, literally.

The main door of his hotel was bedecked with flags and banners welcoming the delegates of the Summit in six languages. Mason had had it checked out. Most of the NATO delegates were staying at the place, and he was looking forward to meeting some old friends later in the bar.

The Warsaw Pact bloc was half a mile away, and the Chinese had taken over a small hotel on the outskirts of the city. He had four hours to make his phone calls, read the papers, and file his first column, setting the scene for the Plenary Session tomorrow; if only he could get rid of the image of that baby with the burned face.

At six, his column written and in the hands of the telex operator, he made his way to the bar and looked around. The first face he saw was a pleasant one. He went up to her, and they shook hands.

"What brings you here?" he asked.

"Jack Mason sent me," said Anna, "to make sure you were keeping your side of the bargain."

"I suppose I should be annoyed."

"Are you?"

He smiled and called over the barman. "Not in the slightest," he replied. He liked the woman. It had been a year or two since they had met, and he was glad to see her. He wouldn't have to explain to Anna Brompton what the Bilderberg Club was.

No one knew who had organized the pilgrimage of the cripples. There were no special buses or trains, no leaders or spokesmen, no banners to identify them, just a mass of crumbling humanity.

When the first of them had taken up position in St. Peter's Square, they had been ignored, the local people giving them a wide berth, out of either politeness or disgust. The police made no attempt to move them on. It was as if they were invisible.

As their numbers grew, they could no longer be ignored, and by the fourth day they had taken over the entire square and started filling the side streets. There was not a whole man, woman, or child among them. If they had not lost a limb or an eye, then they were severely scarred by burns. Anyone with a full set of limbs and clear skin would have looked out of place.

That evening a few reporters tried to talk to them and make them pose for their cameras, but no one would speak. It was a silent vigil, seemingly without political motive. The reporters were baffled. The cripples did not seem to be picketing the conference or trying to attract the attention of the politicians or the Vatican. They were just there, thousands of them, in silent communion.

The only common link was their Semitism. Jews and Arabs. It was obvious even to the humblest observer that they had one thing in common: They were victims of the holocaust, the survivors of the War of Armageddon.

In his limousine taking him to Pereford, Bill Jeffries checked his watch. Fifteen minutes with Damien, then on to Heathrow. He was on schedule, but nervous as he always was when he had to meet the young man. Buher once told him that he had the same feeling. No one in the world, from President to Politburo Secretary, had the same effect. Damien Thorn, like his father before him, gave the impression of omniscience. Both could grasp a concept instantly, both had photographic memories, and heaven help anyone who screwed up. Jeffries grinned to himself at the blasphemy, then reached for the door as the big Rolls came to a stop with a spit of gravel.

Damien sat by the fire, shivering, staring at the TV screen that showed aircraft arriving at the Rome airport and a procession of motorcades taking the delegates into the city.

He looked up as Jeffries came in and smiled, but the older man thought he looked tired. His skin, always sallow, was prematurely lined, but Jeffries said nothing. It was none of his business.

"You have the reports?" Damien asked.

Jeffries nodded and handed them over in order.

"Simon, Peking." Damien scanned the leather-bound memo, then snapped a finger.

"Braddock, Washington." Again a quick scan, another snap of the fingers for the Moscow report, and it was done.

"Good," Damien said. "It's settled."

There was one more memo from the European desk. Jeffries offered it, but Damien shook his head and turned back to watch the TV.

"Do you want a copy of the agenda?" he asked, but Damien flapped his hand at him for silence and hunched forward in his chair to get a closer look at the screen, which showed St. Peter's Square filled with people. The commentator was talking about a dignified, silent protest, a rally without a name or organization. The scene switched to a close-up of a woman holding a baby to her dry breasts. It seemed to have no discernible features.

"The agenda, Damien . . ."

Again a flap of the hand. "I want to see this pantomime," he said.

The vigil filled the square and stretched down the side streets. Every person who could see was staring in one direction, to the southeast, and those who could not see were being pointed in the same direction. As one, without any order, they knelt, and the square resounded to the sound of crackling bones and the groans of the injured.

"What on earth?" Jeffries whispered.

"A homage to the desolated lands," Damien said. "The fools are praying to their gods. Jews and Arabs, united in their misery."

As they watched, the priests began to move among them, blessing them.

"Like carrion among rotting meat," said Damien quietly, still smiling.

Jeffries lost interest in the television, concentrating instead on Damien, who stopped smiling as his eyes flitted among the crowd. It was as if he was looking for something, going from men to women to children, lingering on a sleeping child, then a young boy twitching in prayer; then he turned and looked at Jeffries.

"Paul Buher once had the nerve to criticize me," he said, "comparing me to my father."

Jeffries nodded, wondering how to respond.

"I had a moment of temptation, you see, but I put it behind me."

Again Jeffries nodded, waiting for an explanation. But there was none forthcoming. Instead Damien turned and gazed back at the crowd. They were looking up now, murmuring among themselves, a groundswell of chants, Jew and Arab murmuring a litany together.

"And the lamb shall lie down with the lion," Damien said sarcastically. "What pap."

The camera zoomed in on an old rabbi with a long white beard. He was murmuring a prayer and cradling a child, rocking it, one hand stroking its scalp.

Damien tensed and sat forward, staring at the screen. The old man looked up at the camera, lips moving, his eyes narrowing as if he had seen something. The moment seemed suspended, as if he and Damien were staring at one another.

Damien smiled. . . .

The old man had been at one with his God, in close communion, praying, like the others, for an end to the despair. He did not ask why it had happened, for the ways of the Lord were mysterious, but he prayed for guidance, asking for the weakness of mankind to be turned into strength, praying that the righteous anger of the Lord be diverted, that each man, woman, and child could be shown the true path.

He prayed that there would be no more tribulation, that the world would enter the time of rapture as had been foretold. And the old man, as he prayed, renewed his faith, making apologies to his God for the malevolence of the earth's rulers, for their bombs and their greed, their moral blindness that had caused so much misery.

Then, in midsentence, he became silent, gazing upward but seeing nothing. He could no longer pray. It was as if someone had pulled out a plug and cut his lines of communication. He looked up and he could no longer see the throng around him. He was alone with a foul odor in his nostrils, the stench of scavengers, of jackals and hyenas and of putrefying flesh.

He shook his head and looked down, then shuddered at the sight of the creature in his arms. It was a beast, an obscenity staring back at him with yellow eyes, reaching for him with tiny claws. The old man screamed, raised it above his head, and threw it from him with all his strength, then turned to run, but the scavengers were clawing at him so that he could not move. They snapped at his ankles and knees, tripping him, and their stench made him choke. Then he was down in the dust and he could feel them at his throat. There was blood in his eyes and his mouth, and he tried to cry out for his God, but there was no sound. He could no longer remember the name of his God. As it grew dark and cold, he knew that his prayers had failed him and that in his final moment he had been deserted.

In the square the chaos spread outward and reached into the streets. No one, except half a dozen who were near the old man, knew how it had started, or why. One moment there was peace, the next mindless violence. Only a few saw what happened, the rabbi flinging the Arab baby away from him and screeching obscenities at it, then turning to run; but he was not fast enough.

As the mother picked up her battered child, the father caught the old man around the knees and brought him down, then began to pummel him. The young man had only one arm, but he used it like a poker, punching the rabbi with hard, fast jabs to the eyes and mouth, and as the old man screamed, two of the Arab's friends from the same village joined in.

The men had seen what had happened. It was the age-old treachery of the Jews, personified in this old rabbi, and they joined with their friend, tearing the old man limb from limb, an eye for an eye, a tooth for a tooth, until he was broken and bleeding, while others, two blind Jews, lashed at them.

The blind men were aware of only one thing, of strident Arab voices declaiming the Jews and of the cries of a rabbi choking in his own blood.

Screaming in rage, they kicked out at the Arabs, fighting back, heeding the words of their leaders, who had told them that the Jewish nation would no longer be passive, no longer wail and gnash its teeth at the atrocities visited upon it by others, be they Aryan or Arab.

The fighting spread quickly, the violence feeding upon itself. The blind and the crippled lashed out, some for no other reason than that they were themselves being assaulted; and so they punched and kicked, clawed and bit, until the square was a caldron of anger. In their madness, some of the young men assaulted the women, their rage turning to lust, their self-control lost, acting worse than animals, and the air was rent with cries of terror and passion in equal measure. . . .

Damien smiled and turned to Jeffries, who was staring open-mouthed at the screen.

"And the Nazarene told them to love their neighbors," Damien said before snapping off the set.

Jeffries looked at him and blinked.

"When's your flight?" Damien asked.

"Three-thirty."

Damien nodded. "The mess should be cleared up by then."

◈§ CHAPTER 14 §◈

JACK MASON CONSIDERED himself immune from deep emotion about news events. It was both a strength and a weakness. He could analyze without the filter of sentiment, yet his women often accused him of being coldhearted. He could see their point but didn't worry unduly; it was his nature. But the TV pictures from Rome overwhelmed him. He was almost in tears when Anna telephoned.

"Were you there?" he asked.

"No. I just saw it on TV."

"What made them do it?"

"Who knows?" Mason thought that she sounded irritable and heartless, but he put it down to a bad connection. "There are all sorts of theories," she said. "Mass hysteria, mass hypnosis. The

171

only thing for sure is that it was started by some crazy rabbi."

"Yes, but why?"

"Who knows?" It was irritation in her voice. "I went down there this morning when I heard, but the square was cordoned off. All I could see was the debris, piles of crutches, bloodstained wheelchairs."

"Jesus," said Mason.

"I don't think He had anything to do with it," said Anna quietly, then continued. "We went to the hospital. They can't cope, it's like pictures of the war all over again, everyone physically and mentally crippled—and before you ask, the latest figures are ten dead, including three children, and scores injured, doubly injured if you know what I mean, seeing as they were all crippled in the first place."

There was a silence while Mason tried to wrestle his mind back to the book.

"Okay, so how are you getting on?"

"Zero. That conference is tighter than a nun's arse, excuse the expression. No way in or out. The delegates are all staying at the hotel, and they never come out."

"You've tried this guy Jeffries?"

"Of course, messages galore. I've done everything except send roses."

"You might try that."

"I'd whore for you if I could, Jack, but there

aren't even hookers getting in there, in case of pillow talk."

"Jesus," Mason said again. "Sometimes I wish I'd never started this."

"The only light in the tunnel is our friend Richard. He thinks he knows an Italian who owes him a favor. He's going to try to get him at the end of the conference."

But Mason wasn't listening. The television was showing a replay of what it called the battle of the cripples, and suddenly the book did not seem all that important anymore.

James Richard was not sure whether to be flattered or annoyed by the attentions of Anna Brompton. He had always considered himself a ladies' man; not that he had ever indulged, although, as he told his colleagues, there was no lack of opportunity, especially on foreign trips. It was just that he was very conscious of his position and the chances of being compromised.

Richard thought his colleagues respected his good sense and was mercifully spared the knowledge that they thought him a pompous bore.

Anna, of course, was well behind him in the journalistic pecking order, but he had to admit she was bright. It was she who had found his weak spot so that she could meet Giovanni that night. He remembered her words: "Surely a man in your position must know someone at the

Bilderberg." The emphasis was on the "someone."

"Well, of course, my dear," he had said. There was someone who owed him a favor, Giovanni of Fiat, and before he knew it, he had called the man and organized the dinner.

In a rare moment of self-awareness, he realized that she had made use of his professional pride, but it did not matter. And so there would be a dinner at the hotel when, by rights, he should have been doing the rounds of the delegates' parties. All that the dinner would lead to would be a hangover, but so what? He deserved a hangover. It had been a hectic few days covering two stories at once and getting virtually nowhere. The communiqués coming out of the Summit were banal, with no clues to be found between the lines. He had made note of all the to-ing and fro-ing between the Summit and the Bilderberg, and it was one-way traffic; the politicians traveled in ones and twos to the club's hotel in the evenings.

First the Americans had gone, then the Russians with the Cubans, then the Chinese. The club members did not venture out, and to Richard, this fact illustrated where the power lay.

He read over his copy again, the final piece, full of supposition in the absence of hard fact. He had added two and two and made eight, but in the final analysis, whichever way you looked at it, there was trouble brewing. The flashpoint had moved from the Middle East, which was now a desert, farther east. It was China versus Russia with America looking on anxiously from the sidelines. If he had not been so professionally detached, he might have been scared, for the conclusion was obvious. It would take a miracle to stop a third world war.

His job done, he decided to enjoy himself. Giovanni was always good company, urbane and witty. And Anna? Anna was a question mark, and, he had to admit, a rather seductive little question mark.

He smiled to himself as he adjusted his bow tie. Behind him the TV flickered, showing one motorcade after another heading for the airport; the delegates going home, the jets taking off, carrying their passengers back to their respective capital cities—and nothing, but nothing, had been achieved.

He sighed and snapped off the set, then headed for the door, thinking of the meal ahead, his mind full of historical images, Nero fiddling while Rome burned, Drake playing bowls as the Armada arrived, the band striking up as the *Titanic* went down. It was going to be that kind of night.

The dinner had been a great success. The food was magnificent, the wine excellent, the waiters attentive but not fussy, the conversation witty but unforced. They had dressed formally, the men in dinner jackets, Anna in a simple black dress that showed a lot of her suntan. She had proved to be amusing and, to Richard's delight, content to let him take the dominant role. It had been decided earlier, despite her protests, that he should pick up the bill—or at least his newspaper would. He enjoyed being the host. It gave him the right, he thought, to take charge of the evening.

Giovanni was a tall, slim fifty-five-year-old who had once been the target of the glossy gossip columns but had disappeared from public life ten years earlier with his second wife.

He had been the essence of charm, flirting throughout the meal with Anna, but not offensively, and he had laughed at Richard's stories. But now it was midnight and well into the rounds of brandies and Sambucas, and the Italian was wilting, slightly slurring his speech and leaning too close to Anna.

It was he who had steered the conversation toward the tragedy in St. Peter's Square, and Richard had to change the subject.

Then suddenly Giovanni sat back in his chair and grinned. "Do you know why they threw the leper out of the leper colony?"

They didn't.

"Because he kept dipping his bread in his neighbor's head."

Silence, then Anne closed her eyes and groaned.

"Christ," said Richard. "That's awful." What had gotten into him? he thought. Brandies, he realized.

The Italian was immediately full of apologies and offered to go home. But Richard wouldn't have it. So far, it had all been small talk, but he had not forgotten the object of the exercise, his pact with Mason.

An hour later the waiter was lighting Anna's fifth Sambuca.

"Reminds me of a young reporter," said Richard. "Forget his name. Trying to impress the editor, he ordered one of those, didn't realize you had to blow the flame out, lost his mustache and his credibility. . . ."

By this time the waiters were looking surreptitiously at their watches and Giovanni was talking of going to bed.

"One for the road," said Anna brightly. "My room."

Giovanni swallowed a yawn, and Richard watched him keenly. The man was out on his feet, but his macho pride wouldn't let him refuse. The trick was to get something out of him before he became incoherent.

By two o'clock Richard was ready. This was what he was good at—subtly extracting information. He often compared his job to that of a fisherman. You had to wait until the right moment to haul in your catch. The bait, in this case, had been booze, and Giovanni was ready to be taken.

"I expect the Chinese will be back for the next Summit," he said

Giovanni belched. He was confused, thinking of Anna, wondering which of them she wanted, or was it both?

"No chance," he replied without thinking. "The Thorn people have seen to that."

Richard pretended not to be interested, turned his back on him.

"Ah yes," he said. "Bill Jeffries. I've met him."

Giovanni grunted some Neapolitan oath from his youth. "Jeffries is only the message boy. It's the young Thorn. He's the one. How do you say? The spider in the ointment."

Anna chuckled. "I've heard about him. He's something of an enigma, isn't he?"

"Enigma!" Giovanni roared. "He's a blasted nuisance. He's got the Chinese in his pocket, something to do with quotas of soya or something. You know the Thorn motto, don't you? If you control the food you get the bread—"

"The profit lies in famine," Richard replied as if in religious response.

"Soya," said Giovanni, making the word sound like an oath, then shrugged. "What no one understands is why they are causing the trouble. It makes no sense, economic *or* political." Again he shrugged and lay back in his seat. His little speech had exhausted him. He was so tired that he did not notice Richard leave, nor did he notice a few minutes later that Anna followed him, taking the brandy bottle and two glasses with her.

At the foreign desk of Richard's newspaper, the night man was about to go off duty. In another half hour the last-edition time would be reached and he could get a Victoria cab home to the suburbs.

The phone rang. He frowned into it, asked the caller to speak up, then gestured to the back bench where the editor was sitting. The man walked over slowly.

"Jim Richard," said the desk man. "Pissed."

The editor took the phone, and within moments his frown was identical.

"Listen, Jim, this is Bill." A pause. "Your fucking editor."

He listened for a moment, then shook his head and handed the phone back.

"Garbage," he said. "Some nonsense about World War Three. He's as drunk as a rat."

"What'll I do?"

"Hang up," said the editor.

Half an hour later, in a bedroom in Richmond, the phone rang and Eva Richard twitched, startled out of a deep sleep, to reach for the phone and mumble a hello.

The sound of sex throbbed through the receiver. She shivered and was about to hang up when she recognized the man's voice. It had been a long time since she and James had made love, but there was no mistaking his voice. She trembled as she held the receiver in front her, looking at it as if it were a television set, holding it as if it were glued to her fingers, listening to a woman urging her husband to do unspeakable things, and to James doing them.

Slowly she replaced the receiver and sat still, staring into the darkness for a full minute before the hysterics began.

James Richard surfaced through layers of pain and confusion, blinking at the dawn.

At first he thought it had been a nightmare, erotic to be sure, but a nightmare nonetheless, and that soon he would wake up in Richmond with Eva and get dressed for the office—a place where he was respected, a place where he had never insulted the editor. Then he saw the lipstick smeared halfway down the sheets, and felt the scratch marks on his back.

He groaned, turned over, and saw the receiver lying on the pillow. Again he closed his eyes, knowing that he was lost, a displaced person. There was nowhere on earth for him to go, and he could only hope that when the war started, one of the first bombs would land on Rome.

⊸§ CHAPTER 15 §⊸

JACK MASON WAS beginning to fear for his sanity. He could not sleep without pills, and when he slept, nightmares haunted him. Awake, his frustration with the research was feeding on itself, occasionally turning to panic. He could not concentrate and whenever he tried to be rational, he kept stumbling over biblical references. The problem was that one part of his brain wanted to accept them.

The more he looked at it, the more sense it made. The Jews' return to Zion had been predicted. But the rest of the prophecy was crazy, that after the Jews had returned, Christ would be reborn and meet his Antichrist at Armageddon.

Madness. Wasn't it? Of course it was, but he couldn't leave the idea alone.

The rational part of him rejected it completely. It had to be nonsense, for once the idea of some divine activity was accepted, then there was no point in striving for anything. If everything was preordained, if the human race was a collection of puppets fought over by a deity, be it benign or malicious, with the strings set to be cut at any time, then there was no reason to do anything but wait. Unless our destiny was in our hands, he told himself, there was no point.

All this Antichrist stuff was absurd. So why was he making himself ill?

He paced the room feeling like a caged animal, then stopped at the word processor and the pile of books, notes, and cassettes. In a rash moment, he had bought annotated tapes of the Bible, each paragraph bearing a note of explanation.

He switched the machine on and pecked at it, starting at the end and working backward, checking his notes as he did so.

> And I saw an angel come down from heaven, having the key of the bottomless pit and a great chain in his hand. And he laid hold on the dragon, that old serpent, which is the Devil, and Satan, and bound him a thousand years . . ."

Mason hit the keys, tapping out the word "reference." Then he stood back and read.

Probably symbolic, although some take it to be precise. Refer to 2 Peter 3:8.

The screen went blank briefly as the machine made the appropriate selection, then came up with the verse:

> But beloved, be not ignorant of this one thing, that one day is with the Lord as a thousand years, and a thousand years as one day.

Mason moved to the keyboard again, but the machine had found a dynamism of its own, picking up references and finding the relevant verses.

> Revelation, 20:7,8.

It was a quotation he knew by heart.

> And when the thousand years are expired, Satan shall be loosed out of his prison, and shall go out to deceive the nations which are in the four quarters of the earth, Gog and Magog . . ."

The notes referred to the Old Testament, and the words of the prophet Ezekiel flashed up on the screen:

> And the word of the Lord came unto

me, saying, Son of man, set the face against Gog, the land of Magog . . .

And the notes beneath:

Gog of the land of Magog, the prince of Rosh, Meshech, and Tubal. Rosh may well be the origin of the word "Russians."

Mason sighed and hit the keys once more, going back to Revelation.

In the vision of Ezekiel, Gog of the land of Magog and his confederates come up against the Holy Land and people; but they are slaughtered with immense destruction and Israel is troubled no more.

"Troubled no more," Mason said aloud. "A desert—the peace of the dead."
The machine continued with annotations.

John under similar imagery to that of Ezekiel, describes the third and last great effort of the enemies of the church to destroy her.

"Third and last," Mason muttered. "After Armageddon, the last effort."

He turned away, his head aching with the effort to concentrate.

The screen glowed at him, and he glowered back at it, then checked the notes and punched in a number.

Anna's death list came up, and as he looked at the names, he realized he was shivering. He always seemed to be cold these days. Cold and feverish. Sometimes he felt like a child, afraid of his shadow and things that went bump in the night.

An idea came to him as the list came to an end. He tried to force it away, but it stuck, a limpet on his imagination. He would ask the damned machine a question, get it to do some work for him, get some value for his money.

He selected from the list those whom he knew had investigated the Thorns.

Haber Jennings, photographer; decapitated by a pane of glass.

Carl Bugenhagen, archaeologist, and Michael Morgan, photographer; both buried alive.

Joan Hart, journalist; road accident.

Father Thomas Doolan; buried alive.

Michael Finn, biblical scholar, aviation accident.

To each name he added a period of time they had been working on the Thorns. He made it up. It was just an exercise, after all. He was just playing games.

Then he tapped out two names:

Anna Brompton, researcher.

Jack Mason, writer.

"Okay," he said aloud as he hit the keys. "Let's have a projection. How long have we got to finish our work?"

The words came up:

> Anna Brompton: two days.
> Jack Mason: two days.

"Just a game," he said and smiled to stop the tremor of panic and irrational fear he felt rising in him.

"Screw you!" he shouted at the screen. "what do you know? Goddam machine."

The screen went blank, and he could see his face reflected in it. He stepped back, wondering what the hell was wrong with him, a grown man yelling at an inanimate object to camouflage the spasm of terror he had when he saw an intimation of his mortality. A thirty-thousand-dollar prediction of his death.

He stepped forward again and raised his hands as if to lash out at the machine, then rested his fingers on the keyboard.

"Come on, you bastard!" he yelled. "You've got all the information. The Book of Revelation. Peter and Ezekiel and John and all the rest of them. Give me an answer. What next?"

His fingers danced on the keys. Five words glowed back at him.

The end of the world.

Jack Mason began to laugh—at first just a chuckle, then a belly laugh, until he began to choke. When he had recovered, he sat down and reached for the bourbon.

"Lord God Almighty," he said. "The end of the world. After Armageddon, World War Three. . . ."

He leaned against the keyboard and laughed, his fingers resting on it at random, and when he looked up, he saw the words of the psalm, blinking at him:

> The Lord is my shepherd; I shall not want . . .

And he began to sing, at first quietly, then lustily, as he had done when he was a boy in the Presbyterian church in the Catskills, remembering the hard pews, the minister's stern face, a man whose name he could not remember, the sting of his stick across his palms when he had giggled during a sermon.

He always associated the church with pain. Somehow it was all about pain. Christ on the cross was the ultimate in pain and suffering, and somehow the promise of the Resurrection was a poor compensation for all that agony, a pale postscript. He had rejected the promise of the Resurrection when he reached his teens. He had put away childish things, renounced the teachings of Christ, thinking it all irrelevant.

But now, he sang the old hymn based on the psalm.

". . . in pastures green, he leadeth me, the quiet waters by."

When he had finished, he whispered an amen and closed his eyes, feeling at peace for the first time in a month, but he knew it would not last. It was just an interlude.

Anna had phoned to say she would be arriving at two that afternoon, and Mason decided to meet her at the airport. He wanted out, away from the hotel and the machine that was driving him crazy.

The taxi driver and his radio playing, soft music that was interrupted every few minutes by the banal mutterings of a disk jockey.

The noise made Mason sleepy, and he settled back to relax, trying to blank out his mind. It would be better not to think, just get through life with a closed mind. But the task was beyond him. Anna's list kept forcing its way back into his thoughts, and with it, George's warning that Damien, like his father, had the power over the minds of men and women. He could induce hallucination and madness. The power of evil was almost unlimited.

Mason remembered a name on the list. Andrew Doyle had been U.S. Ambassador in London and had committed suicide in his office. It was a bizarre inexplicable death. There was no note, no possible reason, just the words of his staff that he had been under strain for some time; within a week the new ambassador had installed himself.

Damien Thorn.

Again, for the hundredth time, Mason cursed his rampant imagination. He was being unprofessional and unscientific. It would not do. He had to sober up mentally, and fast.

There was a quiz show on the radio now, three women competing for a holiday in Greece, then an interruption for a newsflash, one of the contestants cut off in midsentence.

Unconfirmed reports said that the Chinese had invaded Taiwan. The Chinese ambassador had been called to the White House, and the Security Council of the United Nations was expected to meet in an emergency session.

"More bloody trouble," said the taxi driver as the newsflash ended and the quiz show resumed. Mason whistled softly, the shock of the news turning his mind to trivial matters, wondering maybe if the quiz was recorded, then deciding it probably wasn't. The players wouldn't care, as long as the Greek holiday was being dangled in front of them. What did it matter what happened to a few million Chinese? They probably thought that there were far too many of them anyway.

Anna was waiting for him. Her flight had arrived ahead of schedule, and when they embraced, he stepped back. She smelled of old booze. Her eyes were hidden behind dark glasses, and the rest of her face—what he could see of it—was camouflaged by makeup, hiding the ravages of a long night.

"I feel as rough as a bear's bum," she said, and Mason blinked. The phrase did not fit the woman. A bear's bum indeed. But before he could say anything she was leading him toward the coffee lounge looking for a quiet table, and reaching in her bag. By the time he had come back with the coffee, she had produced a tape recorder and a small earpiece.

"Couldn't get near Jeffries," she said, "but listen to this."

He fitted the earpiece and snapped on the machine, grimacing at the sound of a drunk, babbling a rambling story about China first invading Taiwan as a diversion before the bulk of the army crossed the northern border and advanced into the heart of Russia. The phrase "population explosion" stammered out of the Italian, then something about soya, about the events being orchestrated by the Thorn Corporation—at least Mason thought that the word was "orchestrated." The man was so drunk that it came out backward.

It was a remarkable calendar of events with a preordained conclusion.

Mason pulled the earplug out and looked at Anna. He asked her what had happened and listened as she told him.

"And what about Richard?" he asked when she paused for breath.

Anna shrugged. "Wasn't down to breakfast. Wasn't on the flight."

So what? thought Mason. The man wasn't important.

"I suppose you've heard," he asked, "about Taiwan?"

She nodded and yawned. "The end of the world is nigh," she said, and for just a moment, Mason thought he caught a glimmer of a smile on her lips.

George's notebook had talked about the Thorn plans for Taiwan, and Mason had dismissed them as insane. Now he remembered his promise to pray for the old man, and for some strange reason it seemed important to him—not only to pray for him, but to pray for Anna, and himself, and just about everyone else on the planet.

As the cab headed toward Knightsbridge and the Hilton, Mason looked left and right until he saw what he wanted, a small church in a side street. He told the cab driver to stop. Anna was asking what on earth he was doing, and once they were on the pavement, he told her about George and his promise.

"Come with me," he said, but she shook her

191

head violently. Whatever color there was in her cheeks had gone, and she was trembling, gazing over his shoulder at the church spire. He turned and followed her gaze, saw her staring at a stone crucifix, her lips moving soundlessly.

"Come on, Anna," he said again. "It can do no harm. At the very least it can—"

She pushed herself away from him so violently that she stumbled back into a lamp post. Mason reached for her, saw the crucifix reflected in her sunglasses. She was clasping her hands as if in prayer, squeezing the index finger of her right hand.

"Anna, what the hell is wrong?" he shouted at her, trying to startle her out of whatever was upsetting her.

He was about to slap her face when she turned and ran, her handbag smacking against the lampost. The tape recorder switched on, and Mason watched her run across the road, heedless of the traffic, the voice of a drunken Italian gurgling at her side, predicting the end of the world.

First amnesia, now this. He had not realized she was so violently atheistic. Maybe once she had had a few hours' sleep she would be okay. He decided to leave her alone for a while before checking on her. Right now he had a promise to keep.

An hour later Mason was back in his hotel, feeling calmer. The fifteen minutes in the church had proved to be therapeutic, and the realization amazed him. If he, professional skeptic and lifelong agnostic, could be soothed by prayer, then what of the believers? He envied them.

He let himself in and started to cross the sitting room, only to stop and blink at the sight that confronted him.

It was as if the place had been struck by a hurricane. His notes were scattered against the far wall and his chair was tipped over. The word processor hummed at him, and as he moved toward it he saw a familiar quotation.

> And when the thousand years are expired, Satan shall be loosed out of his prison, and shall go out to deceive the nations . . .

He cursed and picked up the phone, asked if anyone had been asking for him when he was out.

"Just your assistant, Mr. Mason," replied the receptionist. "I gave her a key. You said it would be all right."

He thanked her, put the phone down, then slowly started gathering up his notes and stacking them in order until the grief and the guilt became too much for him and he slumped to his knees.

It was his fault. If only he'd listened to Harry. If only he'd done the job alone, then she would still be sane.

·§ CHAPTER 16 ࢠ·

IT WAS ALMOST time. Everything that had been written had so far come to pass. There was only the final scene to be played.

In his chapel, Damien, dressed in his cassock, knelt by the altar and prayed aloud to the spirit of his father.

"Our hour has come," he said quietly, "and soon I shall sit at your left hand. The end is almost upon us. The tribes of man are about to unleash the power of destruction. The fall from grace is about to be avenged by the annihilation of the creature made in God's image.

"Mankind has devised the instrument of extinction. He has devolved it and deployed it, that terrible power created by the genius of mankind, a power for good that is about to be made use of for evil."

The young man smiled. "Ever since the serpent, your apostate, seduced Eve, ever since Cain picked up the rock and ended the life of his brother, the end has been inevitable. The Nazarene tried to stop it with His feeble clichés. Love thy neighbor as thyself. Do unto others as you would have them do unto you. Turn the other cheek. Yet in His name, men and women have committed atrocities upon one another. They have died singly, in the thousands, and in the millions for their stupidity, and now comes the ultimate conclusion.

"Had your father not been thrown from the sight of God, had there been no heavenly conflict, then this night of destruction could not have been ordained. It was God who chose the confrontation between the light and the darkness, and soon there will be darkness on the face of the earth for eternity.

"I rejoice, Father. I thank you for giving me the strength to oversee the final days. The power of the Nazarene weakens, but I have witnessed the results. Men I have trusted have been seduced away from me in their last hours, and I pray that their souls may rot in heaven.

"I have known failure, but soon the war will be won. Those who survive the holocaust will not survive the year. There will be floods and hurricanes, the dust will block out the sun, and the living will come to envy the dead."

He slowly got to his feet and gazed down at the altar.

"Soon there will be peace, Father, the peace of a dead world, and your revenge will be complete."

He stretched out his left arm and touched the skull, gazed into the narrow sockets from which his father had surveyed the world, then whispered: "Vengeance is mine, saith the Lord. But revenge is ours."

He turned and strode to the door.

"Let the destruction commence," he said happily.

Throughout the world, the disciples raised their heads and gazed at the sky. The fortunate ones knew that they could go to him and bear witness, while others were content to commune with him from afar in silent unholy prayer. Those who could bear witness left their homes and took to the roads. In a convent in North London, the doors of the cells were opened for the last time.

In Jack Mason's dream he was tied to a cross, his arms stretched along the beam with thick rope binding his wrists; his legs dangled free.

He closed his eyes, and in the blackness could

see the body of Christ on the cross, and he gave thanks for the rope, for surely the nails would have been impossible to bear.

And then there was someone with him. He opened his eyes. The woman was naked, and at first he thought it was one of his wives, but then he saw that it was Anna. She was smiling at him, rubbing him with oil, but the touch of her fingers did not soothe. The oil burned like liniment, and he remembered that they had given Jesus vinegar when he cried out for water. He opened his mouth to protest, but he could not speak, and she moved closer, bit his lips, then moved away laughing, and he felt the blood trickle down his chin.

He looked beyond her into the void and could see nothing. He tried to remember the words of the psalms, but they did not come to him. He wanted to close his eyes and sleep, but he could not do even such a simple thing. He smelled sulfur and tried to think of the name of the Savior but it had escaped him, and he knew that he could not pray to a god whose name he could not remember.

Then she was coming back, and the smell of sulfur got stronger. She was carrying a branding iron, the tip red and smoking.

She stood looking at him, unsmiling, the iron at her shoulder as if she were presenting arms, then she thrust it at his face, and he screamed. The smell of his flesh was like roasting pork, and even as he screamed, even in his agony, he could not help but salivate, and the saliva ran down his chin, diluting the blood from his torn lips. . . .

He awoke in a sweat, hands over his face, his forehead pierced with pain. Trembling, he slipped out of bed and stumbled to the shower.

As the six jets of water hit him, Mason rubbed his chest and thought he felt stickiness, like oil or liniment, and he closed his eyes, afraid of what he might see.

His wrists ached and stung like a nettle rash under the spray, and he forced himself to concentrate, to remind himself of the old man's warning about hallucination. The power of evil could make men and women mad, and he fought against it.

Forewarned is forearmed, he told himself as he stepped out of the shower and went blindly toward the mirror.

He opened his eyes, took a deep breath, and rubbed the steam off. Briefly, for the merest instant, he thought he saw the mark of the brand on his forehead, then he turned on the taps, filled the basin, and threw water at the mirror, clearing away the last of the steam. When he looked again, there was no brand. His face stared back at him, unmarked, and he smiled at himself and thanked God for his strength.

He slept soundly for the rest of the night and woke to the phone ringing. It was Harry, calling from New York. Mason groggily tried to gather his thoughts, wondering what his agent was doing calling at this hour; it was the middle of the night back home.

Harry didn't want to talk about the book. The book didn't matter anymore, now that the Chinese army had invaded Russia. All Harry wanted was to tell him to get the next flight home and quick, before the shit hit the fan.

"Sure, Harry. Thanks."

He snapped on the television. The Soviet news agency, Tass, was describing the Chinese as an army of locusts, and the newscasters were talking about the war plans, how the Russians had threatened many times to annihilate the locusts should they swarm north.

They would deploy tactical nuclear weapons. The old men in the Kremlin had promised and would not go back on their word. It was World War Three, and even the hardened pundits on television looked terrified.

Mason got to his feet and wandered naked into the sitting room, picked up the phone, and dialed Anna's number. The answering machine told him she wasn't at home. She had not left a number where she could be reached.

It did not matter. Mason knew where she would be, and he knew the quickest way to get there. He dialed the front desk.

"Can you hire a helicopter in this town?"

"Of course, sir. When do you need it?"

"Five minutes ago," said Mason, already half dressed and on the move.

❧ CHAPTER 17 ❧

IT WAS TIME.

In single file the disciples moved silently along the corridor to the black chapel and stood for a moment at the door before permitted to enter.

Damien was dressed in his cassock, the dog by his side, and the stigmata bled once more. The ritual was the same for each man, woman, and child. Each one tasted the blood, then moved around the altar to worship at the mortal remains of Damien's father. Some cried. Others were expressionless. One of the nuns almost fainted and had to be helped out by Jeffries, who stood guard at the door.

When the last had gone, Damien picked up the skull of his father and waited while Jeffries placed the bones in a black casket. Then, without looking back, Damien left the chapel for the last time, with Jeffries and the dog close behind. He made his way along the corridor, down the staircase, and across the hall to the main door. Outside the disciples waited expectantly on the lawn.

Damien looked at the congregation and smiled.

"It is written," he said, "that at this hour, those with the mark of the beast shall prosper, while the others will be taken to the bosom of God."

Instinctively some of the disciples made the reverse sign of the cross while others shuffled their feet.

"It is time," said Damien. "Rejoice with me."

A response rose from them, a low murmur: "We rejoice."

"Your loyalty is rewarded."

"We rejoice."

"The end of the world is at hand."

"We rejoice."

Damien waited for complete silence, then stepped out of the house.

"Follow me," he said, "and bear witness."

The crowd made room for him to pass through, then they turned and made their way in single file across the lawn and up the hill toward the church.

It was noon. The clouds were thick and gray, and frost sparkled on the lawn.

Damien reached the withered church sign,

looked at it briefly, and stood by the gate. The others gathered around him, their frosted breath drifting into the church and through the shattered roof so that it looked as if the place were on fire.

"Behold the house of God without a Christian in sight," he said. "Where are they now, Nazarene, when You need them? It is we who are here to mock You and Your Father and Your teachings. It is we who have prevailed."

Then he stepped forward, slowly at first, then quicker, with growing confidence.

"You see, Nazarene?" he shouted at the sky. "I walk upon hallowed ground."

At the door he stopped and gazed inside at the crucifix lashed to the beam, then down at the putrefying corpse beside the altar. He started to walk in but could not do it. He needed the strength of the others, and so he turned and beckoned them into the churchyard.

Like him they were tentative at first, but when they saw that no harm came to them, they ran into the yard among the gravestones, forming a half-circle around him.

Damien smiled at them and moved among them, looking into their eyes, fondling the women, grasping the hands of the men, smiling at the children.

A woman fainted at his touch, and he raised her to a kneeling position.

"Have strength," he said. "Prepare for the final desolation."

The others knelt with her in the frost.

"Wish each other farewell," said Damien, then turned to the east and gazed at the sky, heedless of the murmurings around him and the sound of children crying. He clasped his hands across his chest and closed his eyes.

At first the noise was indistinct, a low rumble above the clouds, then it grew louder and sharper. Damien paid no attention to it until it was almost upon him and the wind was fluttering the cassock so that he had to grasp it tightly around him.

A woman screamed, and Damien opened his eyes, stared straight into a bright light, and ducked instinctively as the sound passed over him. Then he turned and looked down at the house. He was shivering and his arms wrapped around his body while the others looked up at him waiting for his instruction.

Mason was out of the helicopter before the rotor blades had stopped turning, telling the driver to wait for him. He stood for a moment by the lawn, glanced at the house, then looked up the hill toward the church.

He had caught just a brief glimpse of the young man as the helicopter flew overhead, but it was enough. He knew that face in the beam of the light, blinking up at him. The son was the image of the father. There could be no mistake, and as they had flown over the church, Mason had to fight the temptation to keep going, to get away from this place. All his instincts told him to leave, but his curiosity was too strong.

He had no choice. He had to find Anna, but it was more than that. He had to confront the core of his obsession, even if it was the last thing he did.

The crowd rose to its feet as he reached the church. At a rough guess there must have been two hundred of them, all ages, all glaring at him. He briefly scanned the nearest faces, looking for Anna and hoping he would not see her, hoping that he was mistaken.

They parted to let him through, and Mason moved quickly, back straight, head held erect, determined not to show his fear. But it was like confronting a pack of hounds, and he knew they could smell his terror.

Damien stood by the church door with the dog at his side. Mason had to force himself to continue, and Damien stepped back, gesturing toward the church.

"Another feeble emissary." His voice was polluted with sarcasm. "Even at the final hour, the Nazarene will not concede defeat."

Mason stepped past him, unable to look Damien in the face for fear of what he might see. He stopped at the door and gazed inside.

Everything was in focus now. All that he had

read was laid out before him, the bloodstained crucifix with the seven daggers embedded in it, the body of the old man beneath it.

Mason felt sick, and he had to hold on to the doorway for support. Yet despite everything, he still could not bring himself to believe. His whole life had been a search for reason, the unraveling of mysteries, and even now he fought to find an answer, something rational in which to believe.

Behind him, Damien sneered, "What's it to be, Mr. Mason?"

He forced himself to turn and look into Damien's face, tried to recall the words of the psalm, but he could not remember.

"Try," said Damien. "I challenge you. Try to convince any one of them here with the power of your argument. Try to show them the true path. Try to convince just one of them. Where the Nazarene failed, do you think you can succeed?" He laughed. "Just one, Mr. Mason."

Mason looked around at the faces staring blankly back at him, and he shook his head. Vaguely he registered the young man's triumphant voice.

"Nine out of ten came to me through lust," he was saying. "The human race is so predictable. Nine out of ten. A few were attracted by argument, but mostly it was lust. The mark of the Beast, Mr. Mason, is appropriate." Then Mason was aware of someone being led toward him, a woman in a cassock and cowl. Her face was hidden, but he knew before the cowl was lifted who it would be.

"The latest of our recruits," Damien was saying. "She was an easy convert. She knew the background. She had been conditioned as a child by the lies of the Nazarene. These are always the easiest to mold, those who have been well taught."

Anna looked up at him and smiled, her face painted like a whore, and Mason sagged against the door.

A little nun was holding Anna's hand, and she smiled at him. "She came in search of something, and we showed her the way," she said.

Mason called out her name, but Anna turned away from him and smiled at the nun. "Seek and ye shall find," she said. Then she was laughing, a high cackle, and Mason knew he could not reach her.

Damien had tired of the charade. He turned to Mason. "Go meet your Maker," he said. Mason slowly wandered down the nave and stared at the crucifix, then stepped over the body of the old man. It stank. Somehow the clothing made the sight and smell of it all the more obscene—the tailcoat and the wax collar, the bow tie tight around the bloated neck. Maggots squirmed in the eyeballs and around Mason's feet. He shuddered and retched into the dust, again and again, and when there was no more, he went on his knees and prayed, trying to ignore the laughter of the creatures behind him.

It was a baby who began the debauch. Hungry, it reached for its mother's breast and began to suckle, and a group of young men became aroused. Mason could see their excitement and was disgusted. It was a perversion of nature to be aroused by such innocence, and he turned away as they reached for the women nearest them.

At first it was just a small group, then the passion spread and soon the air was filled with their cries, a screeching disharmony of copulation.

Through the doorway Mason could see Damien standing back from it, as if unaware of what was going on. Mason stood up. He could see Anna on her knees in one of the groups, and he closed his eyes in shame. Even as he was repelled, he felt desire for her, an animal desire that could not be ignored. He was so ashamed that he could not look up at the crucifix.

If the priest was right and Christ was walking the earth once more, then Jack Mason knew that he would be too ashamed to seek His forgiveness.

When he opened his eyes he saw an old man pick up a piece of flint and began to hack at the crumbling stone. Soon those without sexual partners were doing the same. The mortar had long since crumbled and there was nothing to stop them. As Mason watched, they tore the place apart, their hands bleeding, tearing down the house of God, stone by stone.

Damien laughed and stepped over the rubble. The others followed him, whooping and crying out obscenities while Mason cowered by the altar. But they ignored him. He was not important, and he knew it. In his final hour he had become irrelevant.

Again he closed his eyes, and when he opened them he saw Anna kneeling beside him, leering at him, her makeup smeared across her face, her cassock ripped and soiled.

She was reaching out for him, murmuring at him to take her, to join them in the last hour. A memory of his nightmare flashed through his mind, and he hit out at her, intending to slap her face, to shock her out of her madness, but she turned toward the blow at the last moment and the heel of his hand smashed into the bridge of her nose.

He felt it break, saw the blood flow, and stood over her as she groveled at his feet.

"Anna," he whispered. "Please."

When she looked up, she was blinking at him, as if awakening from a dream.

"Jack?" Her head cocked, puppylike, frowning at him. One hand lifted to her face while the other pulled the cassock over her breasts to cover her nakedness.

He reached for her, but he was too slow.

Others smelled her blood and pushed between them.

"Anna!" Mason roared. He tried to reach her but was grabbed from behind, one arm held twisted behind his back. With his free hand he lashed out, kicked at the heads as they rushed him, but there were too many, and they forced him to his knees, their breath foul, their bodies rancid with sex. His face was pushed into the dirt so that he could barely hear Anna's screams as they dragged her away, the screams turning to muffled sobs and then, worst of all, to silence.

The scavengers had smelled blood and had acted true to their nature.

It was over. They released him, and he slumped against the altar, looking up at Damien's smile of triumph. He knew that the young man was right. Mankind was finished. The human race no longer deserved to exist, and for the first time in his life Jack Mason welcomed the idea of death. He just hoped it would be quick.

They had virtually torn the place down, and all that remained was four low jagged walls, and the two buttresses holding up the joist. Above him on the altar, an old man was copulating with a child, but Mason took no notice. He had seen too much and the anesthetic of shock had taken effect. He was numb, and took no notice of Damien walking toward the altar and ordering the old man to stop. He only vaguely registered that a thin, pale man with gray hair was bringing a casket to the altar. Damien took the bones from it and laid them on the altar, they knelt in silent prayer, the others following his example until there was silence in the church.

Nothing moved. Their passion was spent, and there was nothing left to do but commune with their spiritual leader.

Mason looked at the shattered doorway. He could escape while they were worshiping, but there was nowhere to go and no one with whom he wanted to share his last moments. It was a terrible fate, to die among these abominations. He allowed himself a brief moment of self-pity, wondering what he had done to deserve this.

Then Damien was getting to his feet. Gesturing to the others to remain on their knees, he turned and looked up at the crucifix, and when he spoke, his voice was triumphant.

"It is over, Nazarene. I no longer feel your power." He smiled. "It is written that Satan shall deceive the nations which are in the four corners of the earth, but it is not deceit. It is their destiny, the ultimate fate of self-destruction. Mankind has chosen. It has rejected your sanctimonious promises of eternal peace."

He turned and surveyed his disciples.

"Look at them, Nazarene. They grovel before me, soiled with the slime of their lust." Briefly he paused, scanning each face.

"I will see you all in hell," he said, and a chorus of amens greeted his promise.

Then he turned and gazed at the bones on the altar.

"Hallowed be *thy* name," he said. *"Thy* will be done, Father. *Thy* kingdom come, on earth as it is in hell."

"Amen," they said.

"For thine is the kingdom, the power and the glory."

"For ever and ever," they responded softly.

"Amen," said Damien.

For a moment there was silence. The congregation was holding its breath so that the sound of laughter, when it came, seemed out of place.

They turned as one and stared at the woman in the doorway. She was wearing a white tunic and carrying a silver urn, holding it out before her as she walked up the nave. She stared at Damien, seemingly oblivious to the others.

"I have the mark," she said, "and so I should be welcome here."

Damien's eyes narrowed, and he leaned back against the altar as she approached.

"For years I worshiped you," she said, then spun around addressing the congregation. "I lay with Paul Buher. I bruised my breasts; isn't that the biblical term?" And again she laughed, a deep chuckle. "I killed for that abomination," she said, nodding at Damien. "Down there in his black chapel. I stabbed my husband to death in my madness, and they tell me that the blood has never been washed away."

She raised the urn high, showing it to the four corners of the church. "These are my husband's ashes, the man I deceived. First I cuckolded him, then I murdered him."

Briefly she closed her eyes and stood as if in prayer, then turned and ran for the ladder, hurdling those in her path. Damien took a step toward her, but then stopped. Mason thought he saw a flicker of confusion, even fear. The dog growled and sprang, but it was too late. The woman had reached the ladder and was climbing fast.

As she got to the top, the skirt of her tunic flared, and the congregation gasped at the sight of her mutilation.

"My God," Mason grunted. Damien turned to him and glared, then moved to the foot of the ladder, looking up as she hoisted herself onto the beam, her legs dangling over the shoulder of the Christ figure. The crown of thorns gouged into her thighs, but she took no notice.

She sat motionless, for a moment, then smiled and kicked away the ladder, laughing at the panic as the disciples tried to crawl out of its path. It smashed into the nave and raised dust, obscuring the crucifix.

When the air cleared, Margaret Brennan was holding the urn high above her.

"You say that your time has come, Damien,

but you are wrong. It is written. After Armageddon, the souls of the dead will be resurrected. My husband will live again. We shall be reuinted."

Damien howled, an animal cry of rage, and scrambled onto the altar. Crouched on all fours to gain momentum, he sprang to his full height, stretching for her, but she was out of reach. When he yelled, he spoke not to her but to the crucifix.

"And still You try to foil me with another dismal convert, yet another lost soul!"

In response Margaret Brennan tore the top off the urn and screamed at him. "Abomination!" Then she twisted and threw the ashes into his face, the sudden movement causing the crucifix to sway and the joist to creak.

A yell of warning came from the congregation, but Damien took no notice. Blinded, he rubbed the ashes from his face, tottered on the altar, then looked up through his tears. Margaret Brennan sneered at him. She rocked the crucifix, gripping the crown of thorns with both hands, screaming the same word, over and over; "Abomination!"

The joist began to crack, and Mason found himself yelling with the others, shouting at Damien to get down, then the joist broke, sending the crucifix plunging face first to the altar. Damien stretched his full height to meet it, arms raised, not to protect himself but to welcome it, screaming in rage, as it crashed into him and threw him back onto the altar, his last sight the mutilation of Margaret Brennan as the crown of thorns ripped through her thighs, then embedded itself in his scalp, the bloodstained face of Christ thudding into his, the body smashing into him and crushing his ribs.

For a moment there was silence, then a long sigh hissed from beneath the crucifix. All that could be seen of him was his arms and legs, wrapped around the body of Christ in a final embrace, his hands and feet twitching in spasm.

Then he was still.

Mason was the first to move. Acting instinctively, he pushed a woman out of his way and wrenched at the crucifix, trying to pull it clear. As he did so, it split along the spine. Grunting with exertion, he pulled it apart, then eased it off the body, shivering with nausea as he pried the head from the young man's scalp. Then it was done and he had to force himself to look at the body.

Damien Thorn glared back at him, a death mask of rage, and Mason took a step back, away from the hands that seemed to be reaching out for him.

The force of the impact had driven the seven daggers deep into his body, and Mason remembered something he had read in the old priest's letter, the instructions from a man named Bugenhagen.

"Each knife must be buried to the hilt, planted

to form the sign of the cross. The first dagger is the most important: It extinguishes physical life and forms the center of the cross. The subsequent placements extinguish spiritual life. This must be done on hallowed ground."

Damien Thorn was gone, in body and in spirit, lying among the bones of his father.

There was one last thing to be done, a testament to Mason's curiosity. He reached forward and wiped away the blood between the fifth and sixth dagger. The old man had been right. There was no navel.

Instinctively Mason crossed himself and turned away as the wailing began.

The disciples crawled out of the church, clambering over the walls, whimpering. The body of Margaret Brennan lay against the west wall, where it had been flung from the crucifix. Mason knelt beside it and pulled down the tunic to preserve her modesty. The skull was smashed, but her face was set in a smile of triumph.

He made his way down the nave and out into the churchyard, stopping by the gate. The dog was digging a grave. Mason watched. The ground was hard with frost, but the dog was strong and determined. When it was satisfied, it crawled into the shallow hollow, settled itself on its side, and closed its eyes.

Mason turned away and looked at the spot where the church sign had stood for four centuries. In their frenzy the disciples had torn it down and smashed it. Mason picked up two pieces and held them in the shape of the cross. As he turned toward the house, he heard his name being called.

Anna was crawling out of the woods toward him, weakly calling to him.

"Thank God," he said. He ran toward her and gazed into her battered face.

"Is it over?" she asked.

Mason nodded.

The tribulation had ended. Now began the time of rapture.

⋞§ EPILOGUE §⋟

ON TELEVISION A panel of scholars asked questions of one another and came up with nothing. Why had the war not followed its predicted course? Why had fingers been loosened from triggers? No one knew, and so they resorted to clichés. Mankind had come to the edge of the abyss and had drawn back in time. At the last moment, sanity had prevailed.

Why? The pundits looked at each other and shrugged their shoulders. It did not matter. It was a time for rejoicing.

Jack Mason snapped off the set and looked at his desk. It was swamped with notes. On top lay a package from Anna with letters and tape cassettes. She'd found it in her file and sent it to him with a note saying that the doctors believed she'd be walking again soon. The mental scars would take longer to heal, they said, but she would eventually be whole again.

The phone rang. It was Barry King, stammering in his excitement, telling him about the birth of a new star in the east.

King had recorded its birth in detail. It was his star. He wanted to know what to call it, but Mason left that task up to him. It was the astronomer's privilege.

He hung up and looked at the sheet of paper in the typewriter, knowing that the first sentence was vital. He knew now how to write the story of the two Damien Thorns. He had all the facts, was surrounded by them. All it needed was inspiration.

He glanced at the old priest's letter, at the prophecy of the man called Bugenhagen who said that there would be many Armageddons. It had happened before and would happen again. Time was circular and there was nothing new under the sun. Mason had found his inspiration. The black star—the birth of Damien Thorn.

"It happened in a millisecond. A movement in the galaxies that should have taken eons occurred in the blinking of an eye. . . ."

Later he would think of a title.

And there shall be no more curse: but the throne of God and of the Lamb shall be in it; and his servants shall serve him: and they shall see his face; and His name shall be in their foreheads. And there shall be no night there; and they need no candle, neither light of the sun; for the Lord God giveth them light: and they shall reign for ever and ever.

REVELATION 22:3-5

Recommended Reading from SIGNET

Medical Thrillers from SIGNET

*Prices slightly higher in Canada

SIGNET Mysteries You'll Enjoy

*Prices slightly higher in Canada
†Not available in Canada

**Buy them at your local
bookstore or use coupon
on next page for ordering.**

Great Reading from SIGNET